RETURN
TO THE
ENCHANTED
ISLAND

RETURN
TO THE
ENCHANTED
ISLAND

JOHARY
RAVALOSON

Translated by Allison M. Charette

Text copyright © 2012 by Johary Ravaloson
Translation copyright © 2019 by Allison M. Charette
All rights reserved.

Previously published as *Les larmes d'Ietsé* by Éditions Dodo vole in France in 2012. Translated from French by Allison M. Charette. First published in English by Amazon Crossing in 2019. An excerpt from this book was previously published in *Tupelo Quarterly,* no. 9.

Excerpt from page vii of the foreword to *Mood Indigo* by Boris Vian, as translated by Stanley Chapman, reprinted by permission of Farrar, Straus and Giroux.

Published by Amazon Crossing, Seattle

www.apub.com

Amazon, the Amazon logo, and Amazon Crossing are trademarks of Amazon.com, Inc., or its affiliates.

ISBN-13: 9781542093538 (hardcover)
ISBN-10: 1542093538 (hardcover)
ISBN-13: 9781542093514 (paperback)
ISBN-10: 1542093511 (paperback)

Cover design by David Drummond

Printed in the United States of America

First edition

Only two things really matter—there's love, every kind of love, with every kind of pretty girl; and there's the music of Duke Ellington, or traditional jazz.

Everything else can go, because all the rest is ugly— and the few pages which follow as an illustration of this draw their entire strength from the fact that the story is completely true since I made it up from beginning to end.

Boris Vian
Foreword to *Mood Indigo*
1947
Translated by Stanley Chapman

PREFACE

A friend, who didn't understand what I was always scribbling in my notebook and who missed the elders' oral stories, recited a *hainteny* to me, a poem-turned-proverb:

"Vato hanasan-damba, ny lamba lasan'ny tompony, ny ranon-tsavony lasan'ny rano, ny vato mijanona eo ihany." (In the wash-house, the clothes leave with their owner, the soap with the river water, and the rock remains.)

"Ponder it well," he said to me. Then he added, "No one writes any modern hainteny."

Thus, in the following few pages, I would like to offer up these two expressions:

—*Men do not cry; they are contemplating Ietsy's pool.*
—*Enchanted as Ietsy was, buried in the land of his children.*

For this prodigious task, I necessarily called upon a name out of legend. If my friend will accept these two phrases as rock, the rest of it, "completely true," may leave with the river water.

Trois Mares, July 29, 2005

THE ENCHANTED ISLAND

For some time now, even though there was likely nothing that should have disturbed his nights, Ietsy would wake up. Usually, at such moments, there were no crickets chirping, and no owls hooting. The pipistrelle bats had apparently paused their furious fluttering, and their furless wings neither made striking flap-flap sounds nor beat the air. There wasn't even a breeze that might have crinkled the leaves on the trees, not even slightly. The normal wooden creaks of the house were silent. No restless stirring could be detected beneath the bedsheets. It was as if the silence itself had pulled him from his sleep.

Should it continue, he'd persuade himself that he was sleeping, dreaming, keeping his eyes shut and not moving a muscle. He'd let his mind wander, grasping at profound or asinine thoughts here and there but never pushing them through to their conclusions, so as not to chase off his almost-dreams.

Surely, the echoing lull—or rather his passing isolation—would never last long enough for the wandering to persist.

Certain sounds did ebb and flow like a lazy tide, with a few popping abruptly in his auditory canals. The ones that never ceased, like the one from the regulated movement of the hundred-year-old pendulum set into the wall above the staircase. It was so much a part of the house itself, aging with it instead of measuring the passing time, that sometimes you could forget entire days even as it chimed each quarter hour and ticked every second. His wife's breathing, so regular and so familiar that he had to concentrate to discern her presence, so close, almost inside, breath of his breath—he'd been married to Lea-Nour for over fifteen years—it made him fall in love all over again. Dogs started barking again nearby. An echo reached him of a truck passing on the national road; a buzzing insect or gnat irritated his ear. He picked out the sound of a spider's eight legs brushing against the baseboards, the muted sound from the next room of the sleigh bed's feet against the mildly warped wood as his youngest child tossed and turned, the sighs and murmured half phrases of children's dreams from his oldest daughter or her sister in the room down the hall, the crumpled garbage bag in the kitchen downstairs with probably a mouse or roach digging jumpily through it, and the wind tousling the slumbering outdoors.

During these moments, if he did lift his eyelids, he would remark that it was, unsurprisingly, dark. As his pupils dilated, he could make out an arm, if his wife had rolled over in her sleep, or part of her back, her face faintly aglow from the white sheets, and other forms, also blurry, of unmoving objects that seemed to have been there for years.

He could sometimes see a star twinkling through the cracks in the shutters, or the pale clear moon, momentarily covered by the frenetic paths of passing pipistrelles, hunting their thousands of mosquitoes per day. Like them, he could move around the house without light, this house that had witnessed his birth.

He could get up noiselessly and breathe the country air, now so close to the city. He didn't do anything of the sort at first. He wanted to recover his sleep as quickly as possible. Mostly, he didn't want to interfere with the unfolding night.

He knew all this, and it buttressed the calm. The calm of Anosisoa, the home of the Enchanted Island, between the rice fields and the woods, within the centuries-old walls, the calm of the neighboring village, the industrial zone, the city, places a hundred miles in every direction, probably the entire country. All of that was reassuring. All of that should have reassured him. It should have created a state of peace, but that state here wasn't known as *sleeping at night*.

His nocturnal disquiet may have had something to do with his inactivity during the day.

Ietsy Razak didn't have what one would call a career, much less a job. Granted, he didn't have to worry about what he would eat, how he would clothe himself, where he would live. All material concerns had been provided for him, in advance and in abundance.

It had always been like that in their family, as far as I know.

First, Ietsy the Blessed One, the Great Ancestor. And then the forebears of Ietsy Razak who had crossed thousands of nautical miles to reach this land set among the waves. To complete their journey, they'd walked on giant lily pads floating on the ocean. Once on the island, they'd worked deftly to make the effects of their enchantment last from generation to generation. They replaced the original masters of this land, transforming their existence into myth by integrating them, conquering them, or driving them to the wilder ends of the earth. They wound their way into the delicate, tightly interlaced caste system, asserting their dominance by force, alliances, or more often the timely breaking of alliances. They always supported the kingdom's expansion and took their share of the spoils. They fell in step with later waves of migration, profited from them. Trade made them rich once and for all. They bowed before the colonial forces and demonstrated intelligence, a type of adaptation so close to compromise that the outsiders probably couldn't have told the difference—but even so, they remained among the only ones concerned with defending what the latest arrivals were lusting after. To establish their power under the rising sun of independence, they sowed progress, benefited from the hunger for knowledge, and imposed undeniable authority. They made themselves indispensable in every time, even during the revolution when everyone wanted to fell old trees like them.

Like his forefathers, I should say, for Ietsy Razak only ever reaped the fruits of that history.

And at every rude awakening, business picked back up again. People wanted to farm their lands, lease their buildings, borrow their funds, avail themselves of their wisdom and experience. It all worked, ran by itself like the electric train from his childhood. There were some incidents, of course, but Ietsy's father, Mr. Razak, was a shrewd man. He'd diversified, turned a profit from all his lands, belongings, relationships. People came to consult him on all the important national issues. He kept a firm hold on the family fortune, partially from a passion for power but also because of his only son's complete disinterest.

Ietsy had only simple desires. He only had to ring a bell for the housekeeper, secretary, or administrator to come running, all the old staff to hear and obey—they were all part of the inheritance, the divine and ancestral blessing, surely.

Blessed by the Gods and Ancestors. That was what his father always said when he made young Ietsy give thanks. That, too, was customary. They went to perfume their ancestral tomb, the paternal side in Anosisoa at the new year, his mother's side in Ambatofotsy on All Saints' Day. On every holiday or minorly important occasion, they poured out a drink in the sacred northeast corner of the house, in a small alcove, which had not the ancestral portraits on display—those kept watch over the hallways or held court in the parlor—but symbols representing the ancestors engraved into rot-proof wood (a small old scrap that may have once been the stern of a boat, with mysterious lines on it, nearly entirely erased, but undoubtedly made by a human hand). And they took pride in being the family that displayed the most splendor every seven years or when social norms dictated—an approaching election, or the day before a change in the tax rate when they'd have to call upon their allies—when they rewrapped the *lambamena*, shrouds of wild silks, of those resting in their vaults.

Over the years, the luxury of how they "re-turned" their dead made other families' ceremonies pale in comparison, especially during the enlightened revolution—or at least the first few years, truth be told—when the government tried to discourage extravagant traditions. However, according to Mr. Razak, they always owed their ancestors that, their ancestors who granted them the fullness of their blessing.

They'd always been among the first to receive insights from beyond the seas—science, culture, even the trappings of religion when necessary. Thus, they were now one of the great Christianized families.

They had of course always venerated the land of their ancestors and acknowledged it as the source of all good things. But for a time, they had also designated pork as taboo, to the satisfaction of the Muslim traders, and continued to use their writing style long after people here had forgotten who Muhammad and his god were (after all, Mecca is not on the Enchanted Island). They'd seen the technological superiority of the whites, supported King Radama I in his policy of openness toward the West, and accepted the transcription of the Malagasy language into the Roman alphabet without qualms. When Queen Ranavalona II converted to British Christianity in the nineteenth century, they built the first churches where those who had followed the foreigners' god too early during the preceding reign had been executed.

The stone for the church in the Rova, the royal citadel dominating the capital, had come from a family quarry. The diaconal duties always fell to them. Ietsy was second only to his father to shake the pastor's hand at the end of the service. The Razaks had permanent seats right behind the royal chair carved of hardwood with its scarlet cushion. The throne, long unoccupied but once believed unmovable.

Sadly, a terrible fire had reduced everything within the royal walls to dust, the church, the five palaces: Manjakamiadana, the palace of Queen Ranavalona I and her successors; Manampisoa, the one Queen Rasoherina had added; Tranovola, for Radama I; Mahitsielafanjaka, for Andrianampoinimerina, the father of the

Malagasy nation; and Besakana, for Andrianjaka, the founder of Antananarivo. Up in smoke, too, went what had been discovered of the *trano manara*, the cold-house tomb below which lay the former sovereigns: the Fito Miandalana, or Seven Aligned-Houses. The flames ravaged the sky for an entire night; the city's summit could be seen for dozens of miles. Crowds came from all around to climb the hillsides, larger and still more despondent than a century before when the last queen, Ranavalona III, had departed in exile. Rivers of crashing tears flooded the underneighborhoods; only lamentations rose, and they could not conquer the flaming citadel. Hours later, heat still tortured the cladding of the great palace stones, whose four iconic towers were like giants being burned alive, writhing and roaring without falling over.

Since then, with aid from the international community, more stone had been cut for the church. The trano manara of the Seven Aligned-Houses had been rebuilt, the cold dwelling place of the ones who had reigned over Antananarivo since King Andrianjaka had consecrated the capital with that name, at the end of the Gola era and the dawn of the Zak, in 1610 on the Christian calendar.

"Can money be used to re-create sacred relics?" Lea-Nour whispered to Ietsy at the inauguration ceremony for the first phase of restoration.

"The ancestors do not die!" he whispered back.

She sighed as she looked at those gathered, all dressed in the same clothes: modern yet carefully acknowledging tradition. For the women, a Chanel suit or something that passed for it, a silk *lamba* between white and cream around their shoulders, rarely with the traditional chignon at the nape of their neck, like Lea-Nour; the men in dark suits, some with bow ties, like Mr. Razak, and of course the lambas over their shoulder, white with red stripes—the solid red lambamena befitting only the sovereign or the ancestors, and warriors the only ones permitted to wear the black-banded lamba.

"There's nothing there!" she said.

Ietsy didn't know if she was talking about the people in discourse around them or the tombs. The threat that the vacuity of the former represented, because they ran the country, and the latter, because nature—and especially death—abhors a vacuum, even with the rituals to erase the shame of forgetting the ashes of ashes, could make any elder shudder. But the world was entering the third millennium, and, in the shadows of the stones that still stood, after sacrificing a zebu and consecrating new roofs for the tombs, the rebuilt church was inaugurated.

As for the hardwood chair, other furniture, and the very structures themselves of the Rova's other buildings, they are still waiting for the tears shed that horrible night to water the trees needed for reconstruction, as well as the other emblems of sovereignty.

Before, Mr. Razak had made a habit of bringing Ietsy here to look out over all of Antananarivo, reminding him of their role in making kings throughout the ever-shifting precolonial period and even more so throughout their regained independence. Two eras symbolized ever after by thoughtless renovation and tumorlike growth.

"I don't believe any of it," Lea-Nour said in spite of everything one day, shaking the black hair resting simply over her shoulders.

Ietsy, walking beside her behind the house, watched her jet-black eyes rebel in her wise oval face. The October wind whipped through the warm air, making jacaranda flowers float to the ground. He questioned how anyone could live in the skin of someone who didn't believe any of it. The mauve flowers carpeted the path running straight to the tomb.

"Your father opened all of Anosisoa for me," she said. "Even this vault. Up to now, it was inaccessible for women who married in! I appreciated the gesture, as did my parents . . ."

"Your father was so pleased that Vazimbas were returning to Anosisoa!"

"He always thought of himself as more *vazimba* than anyone else." Lea-Nour smiled. "I'm not really worried about it, though—when it happens, I'll be dead, you know."

"You don't want to become an ancestor?"

"They're just dead people, like God is just Sunday morning tedium. If everyone believed like you do, Ietsy, we'd be able to rebuild the Rova without any foreign aid!"

And she laughed, her large stomach stretching before her, full of happiness.

"You really don't believe it?"

"I believe in life," she said, caressing her belly. "In children. In preserving this earth for our children, enriching it and passing it on. In Filistria. Weren't you the one who told me about Gombrowicz?"

"Yes. Sanctifying the earth is always protecting it. It's dedicated to our children or ancestors."

"Sure." Lea-Nour smiled. "But ancestors live in a tomb, whereas children can travel anywhere they want!"

The Razaks' loyalty, which harbored the same ambiguities as their long history, troubled Ietsy. But only a little—it was only ever a small pebble in his shoe. As a child, he went to the Protestant church on Sundays and to Catholic mass on Thursdays at his school (Sintème, which had overseen the education of his father, grandfather, great-grandfather, and all of the country's elite since colonization). But his father's most essential entreaty was to not forget the great crossing and the source of unending milk and honey. The god on the cross had been welcomed into the traditional pantheon with the others. The Jesuits charged with Ietsy's education nearly turned him into a skeptic, but after enduring several trials, his ancestors' protection proved extremely strong.

He was probably around eleven years old when he saw concrete evidence of it for the first time. The way people in Anosisoa obeyed his every whim obviously didn't count; that came more from their attachment to financial stability than a fear of invisible, wrathful beings harassing anyone who would try to thwart the blessed one.

There was a guy in the grade above him, mixed race, burly, built, a full head taller than him. He acted all tough and unaware of Ietsy's natural birthright. One lunchtime, while the other guy was walking home with a few friends to his white *vazaha* neighborhood next to school, our doubting Thomas sat on the hood of the car and told the driver—often under pressure to shift between Ietsy's desires and his responsibility to the father—to follow them, and to only pass them once they'd gotten a little ways away from the pink brick outer wall of the hallowed school. Ietsy got all fired up by the stares of the crowd as he passed by like in an Independence Day military parade, confirming his divine and ancestral consecration in his heart of hearts even before completing that first trial. Once the car reached the other guy, Ietsy stood up on top of the roof and hurled insults at him. Everyone following behind was too captivated and surprised by the scene to yell at them to clear the road; perhaps some of them had recognized Mr. Razak's car. None of that mattered to Ietsy. He continued his diatribe, calling upon the gathering mob as witnesses to the cowardice of the other guy, who didn't understand the situation fast enough. Then, when he finally opened his mouth, Ietsy jumped him. From the car, he had enough momentum to knock the guy to the ground and pummel him. The driver hoisted himself out of the car and pleaded with Ietsy to stop, while at the same time preventing anyone else from intervening or laying a finger on him, giant that he was. Ietsy left the other guy with blood running down his face.

That afternoon, no one at school talked about anything besides the supernatural trial that had happened. The victim's parents complained to the rector, but he sidestepped the issue: *extra muros*, outside his jurisdiction. During his sermon at that Thursday's mass, he made only a brief allusion to it, staring hard at the blessed one among the rest of his students. Ietsy pretended not to understand.

The young vazaha never had a chance to exact revenge. The driver, in defiance of regulations, started waiting for Ietsy right at the door to his classroom, too afraid that some accident might befall his master's son. The rest of the time, his friend Nestor—whom they called Thor or Néness, depending on if they were emphasizing his strength or klutziness—towered behind him like a real bodyguard. Besides, they were reminded in their studies that violence was a crime, and as the fat headmaster Brother stressed, the punishment—suspension from school—could be permanent.

The following year, the parents of the vazaha boy—*colonie* by default, that was what they called anyone who was forced to tolerate everything that someone else did—pulled him out of Sintème and enrolled him in the French high school. The Gods' and Ancestors' protection fell unquestionably within the realm of perfection.

Three years later, the blessing was confirmed a contrario, as he would later tell it (with linguistic habits acquired on the bench at law school, people might think, as Ietsy was supposed to get his law degree like his father, if they didn't know that his exposure to syllogism dated back to childhood, to long lunches in Anosisoa when, while Mr. Razak and his guests binged on clever debate and florid words, Ietsy and his friends pigged out on food and learned the strange effects of alcohol, Ietsy making a valiant effort after several swigs of the paternal whiskey to stay straitlaced until the soft rays of the setting sun streamed into the room and flooded the white plaster wall before going dark). That year, which would end up being his last at that school, he was less bored: there were girls, and a new kid, Arthur, another mixed guy who'd gone in the opposite direction of the ex-colonie, from the vazaha high school to Sintème, and introduced them to the forbidden world of smoking.

I'm obviously not referring to tobacco—which also wasn't tolerated, outside of the rector's office—but about what no one smokes anymore besides gangs and guys who haul pushcarts, to avoid feeling fatigue. And artists, too, for inspiration—like the new kid's parents.

When Ietsy visited their house, he didn't get a chance to see Arthur's father, a theater man. His mother, on the other hand, a painter—he often caught sight of her in her studio in the back of the garden, from which the scent of the Ancestors' weed sometimes wafted. Art was a foreign milieu for Ietsy; he only knew that the paintings that hung on their walls in Anosisoa, which some of his father's friends drooled dumbly over, were worth a lot of money.

He fantasized more about Arthur's mother, who wasn't just an artist but a redhead too. She was from the north of England, near the Scottish border. Her ancestors had fallen in love with the Malagasy sky as they got closer to it during the era of the London Missionary Society. In the first part of the nineteenth century, the awful Queen Ranavalona I had driven out the religious zealots of the Queen of England beyond the seas, for fear they might win over her own subjects' hearts. By following in their tracks back to the island, Ms. Jones was chasing an old family dream. But of course, no matter how blessed the young Ietsy was, she was naturally out of his reach.

Thursday afternoons in Arthur's room, with no classes, there was Jeannie. She was the most shameless of all the girls in their class, who'd only started to be dropped into high school in their third year, a few at a time. Jeannie was hitting the joint with them, and it had a fantastic effect. She wanted them to touch her, kiss her. The others thought it was funny, especially Néness, and Arthur too; not Ietsy, he'd always been put off by group work. He watched them, or listened to Charlie.

It must be said that *andzamal* causes very weird sensations. The cannabis caused Ietsy, already a naturally contemplative person, to be so engrossed that he could watch flies mating for centuries. As for Charlie, he couldn't stop reading, poems or other books he'd grabbed from the library that lined the hallway to Arthur's room. Sometimes he would unveil the beauty of a text out loud to his friends, but they'd laugh "at anything and everything," he had said, annoyed. Ietsy didn't hear anything very well or feel anything specific, neither agreeable nor disagreeable, as if he were far away, but when the others laughed, he spasmed too, for no apparent reason, and, like the others, sometimes without stopping for an eternity.

Charlie thought they were morons and kept repeating that poetry was the only thing worth anything at all.

"A poet, while the rest of the world wallows and bathes in muck," he told them, "a poet takes a dump standing up!"

The others rolled around laughing, without quite understanding why. It had become a conditioned reflex, even without the stimulus of cannabis. The instant there was the slightest lyrical allusion, they'd exchange glances and laugh hysterically.

They'd had to memorize a poem for French class. The day it was due, the teacher asked for a volunteer to recite it. She was undoubtedly thinking of Charlie. Before anyone else reacted, though, Ietsy raised his hand, suddenly inspired by the text. He'd barely read the title. He wanted to blow everyone away, especially the pretty teacher whose copper-colored hair made him think of Arthur's mother. She didn't let any of her surprise at her student's unexpected enthusiasm show, just invited him to come to the front. He stood in front of her desk so that she could see only his back. Before the class—ready for anything, knowing him—he began his performance. He lowered his eyes, pretending to concentrate, then, staring hard at Jeannie and Arthur with the most constipated expression—he knew there was no point in looking at Néness—he barked, "Invitation to the Voyage!"

His comrades burst out laughing, followed of course by the entire class. He huffed, acting offended but unfazed. Once the room was calm, he started over. He didn't have to make sure they were paying attention anymore. He kept his eyes

19

half-closed and made a face as he intoned the first syllables again, letting the next line tumble out in a rush of relief. And again, to widespread hoots of laughter. He turned around and gave the teacher a mock-hurt look, but of course she hadn't seen anything and was just tapping her pen on her desk.

"Well, go on!" she cried.

He let a few quiet moments pass, then continued his act. Arthur was bent over double from laughing, Jeannie had tears streaming down her face, and Néness was smacking the table and his thighs. Everyone, he thought, was laughing. It was contagious. Even the teacher had a hint of a merry smile as she renounced her plan and told him to take his seat.

As he returned to the back of the classroom, he saw Charlie's strange expression, but riding the euphoric success of a schoolboy, he hadn't thought anything more of it. He just wondered if his friend, too, had been smoking before coming to class.

One afternoon a few days later, Arthur brought over some "super-high-quality" stuff. It was just after Easter, and the rainy season was well over by then. They'd never smoked inside the school grounds. As they were enjoying it in the shadow of the pine trees above the soccer field, the quietest corner at Sintème, the poet of the group took some pills out of his pocket.

"With these," he said, "it will be a spleen explosion!"

They didn't know what that meant. They were already soaring. They'd missed the start of class. Charlie was telling them about his own experiments, the rest of the group was laughing. Ietsy was with them and sometimes with himself. Probably everyone else too. Jeannie, between Néness and Arthur, was touching herself on the blanket of pine needles. When Charlie gulped one of the tablets down and held out his hand with the rest, she took her own hand out of her pants to take one and swallow it. Jeannie certainly didn't have cold feet. Ietsy hesitated. Néness took one, and finally Ietsy did too. Only Arthur demurred. He preferred it au naturel, he said, rolling another joint. No problem, they were open to anything, time had stopped. Then, Ietsy thought, he fell asleep.

Néness was the only one who'd actually slept, Arthur told him later on the phone.

"You guys completely lost it. Especially Jeannie!"

Ietsy had only a faint idea of how they'd lost it. He woke up at home under his bed; he had a headache and felt exhausted. Snippets of scenes were coming back to him, but he didn't know which ones were part of reality. He thought maybe he'd cried at one point, and at another, he'd been naked as the day he was born, racing against an equally naked Jeannie and Charlie.

"All the fathers and brothers in the school were chasing you around the courtyard with blankets," Arthur told him, screaming into the receiver with laughter. "They wanted to get your clothes back on, but you didn't make it easy for them!"

Apparently, once they were corralled beneath the Jesuit inquisitors' eyes, caught and covered—everyone except Néness,

21

who was probably still snoozing under the pines—Jeannie stood up and pissed in the rector's office, singing all the while.

Ietsy didn't remember that at all. He listened to Arthur, shaking with nervous laughter that made him bang his head against the mattress slats. He got a nice bump, but not enough to make him move or think it was any less funny. On the other end of the line, Arthur also cackled with laughter, like during their finest hours.

"We're gonna get kicked out!"

But even that he said laughing hysterically. Neither of them was yet aware of the tragedy.

Ietsy, suddenly hearing his father's heavy footsteps coming up the stairs and then in the hallway, smothered his laughter with his hand and, still under his bed, slammed the phone down and tried to look apologetic. He heard the click of a key in the lock. Mr. Razak walked in, livid, in one of his eternal dark suits, his mustache and goatee unkempt from rage. He wrenched the telephone out of the wall and took it out of the bedroom, his son unable to hold it. The door slammed, and the lock snapped shut.

Ietsy crawled carefully out of his hiding spot, which wasn't actually a place to hide because the old-fashioned bed, too tall and not wide enough, hid nothing from view. He started asking himself what he'd intended, choosing a refuge like that, when the key turned again in the lock.

His father entered, followed by two maids and the house-man, stooped and slow. The master of the house strode over to the wardrobe without a single glance at Ietsy and opened both its doors. The others, their job obvious, scooped up all the clothes they could find, including everything on the floor, the chair, and the desk, bringing all of it outside. Each of them made two trips, the man throwing fearful looks at him as he passed, while the women lowered their eyes, one respectfully and the other, the younger one, hypocritically, unable to keep a smile away from the corners of her mouth. His father stood rigidly before the armoire, as if trying to bore his anger through the sandalwood. Silence hung heavily over the swishing fabric.

Ietsy didn't react, too dumbstruck. He figured he must still be under the effect of the drugs, literally hallucinating. Once his wardrobe was emptied, everyone left and the door was shut, locked again. Then he realized he didn't even have boxers on, and his other things had already been stripped from the room. They'd probably looked for narcotic substances he might have been concealing. But he hadn't reached that point; for him, he was only trying things with friends to have fun. So there he stayed, naked and cut off from the outside world.

The only contact with the outside that his father permit-ted was the plates of food slid in and furtively removed by a wordless, terrified servant, and the old chamber pot that had been used just before his great-grandfather's final days (in his final days, he'd worn diapers, which a nurse changed for him like for a baby). He racked his brain for a good strategy: Would it be better to rebel, scream, throw the pseudoindulgent food against the wall, do the same with the shameful pot and its contents, then jump out the window and leave a scandal outside in his wake, or do everything at the same time? He'd certainly done enough already. Upon prudent consideration, he decided it would be rather dangerous. He was on the second floor, more than twenty feet up; the Razaks had high ceilings. For a moment he decided to bend, try to mount some sort of defense, but nothing came to mind that would ever withstand his father.

After the third day, it was getting to be too long, and he prepared to go on the offensive. But instead of the regular Quasimodo, the housekeeper was the one who poked her head, ageless even back then, through the door of his room around noon. She didn't bring a meal, but clothes.

"Your father is expecting you in the library," she said, her voice as misty as her eyes.

She likely had strict instructions too, because she said only that, then slipped back out and closed the door behind her, but without touching the key this time. He quickly got dressed and mentally prepared himself for war.

His father was playing quite the game, even making him wear his dark suit, the one Ietsy had worn a few months earlier for the funeral of his incontinent elder. He dragged his feet down the stairs. Upon seeing him, his father, in shirtsleeves but a knotted tie, rose from his armchair. Walking toward the living room, he let one sentence drop casually as he passed: "We'll have a quick bite to eat, and then we're going to bury your friend Charlie."

It was as if he'd been struck by lightning. He wondered if he'd heard right. He couldn't believe his ears, but he couldn't hope that it was a joke, either. If it must be spelled out, Mr. Razak was as much a prankster as Jeannie was Mother Teresa. And although he would sometimes laugh with his guests, wielding a type of humor that was not shared with his son, he was not in such a mood that day. Ietsy followed him unsteadily. His head was spinning, his heart racing. His father already sitting and the housekeeper waiting, standing in front of the door to the serving pantry. Water looked like it was trickling down the chandelier above the table. And the light that normally poured in through the high windows had become fuzzy. He didn't realize it was tears, forced out from his eyes without him noticing, blurring the scene until they fell from his cheeks to form clearly visible wet spots on the shining wood floor, brushed daily with abrasive coconut husks and rubbed with beeswax every Friday, the tiniest things in the Razak household often becoming such regular, scheduled routines.

The last time he'd cried like this, he must have been seven or eight years old. For his bad behavior, serious enough that his father promised him a thrashing, he'd been banished from the table and sent to his room to wait. The patriarch had never hit his kid before, but that time, he truly seemed ready to strike.

As he sent him upstairs, he'd added, "I won't take off my belt just yet."

He's going to kill me, the child had thought. His fear had made urine run all the way down his jellylike legs as he climbed the interminable staircase, and his reddened eyes flowed like waterfalls. He kept crying for a long time on his bed. So long that he'd fallen asleep, exhausted. When he'd woken up later in the afternoon, his father had already gone back to work, and he didn't know if the sentence had ever been carried out. He never knew. The housekeeper had never really revealed anything, only grousing that he'd deserved to be punished, and he'd made sure not to question the primary individual.

This time, adolescent Ietsy dared to ask his father a question, choking back sobs: "Are you going to kill me too?"

Mr. Razak didn't reply. Still, setting down the fork he'd been bringing to his mouth, he merely gave his son a strange look. It was clearly very inappropriate.

But Charlie hadn't been killed by his own father, either. At least, not really. His friends whispered during the funeral that the man most likely would have done it, if it would have prevented a scandal. They wondered if murdering his child would have caused the minister of youth and culture less indignation than his son of dying of an overdose. Children of powerful men, no matter what the father's position, were allowed to do anything, even favoring death over life, never mind what the priest said, clearly obligated to focus the mass on the temptations of artificial life.

Arthur had managed to communicate with Charlie shortly before the tragedy. He was locked up and stripped of all his belongings, like Ietsy. His books, his beloved books, they'd taken Baudelaire, Burroughs, and the others from him. His parents believed them to be the source of his insane debauchery.

"Even Rabearivelo, a national treasure!" added Arthur, who now saw himself as the only one with any knowledge of such matters, because of his artist parents.

Charlie's misfortune was still having a key that opened every door in the house, particularly the one to his parents' bedroom, where he'd gone to procure the pills for his final trip.

Arthur's mother, who'd also come to the burial, refused to join the line to shake the hands of "those people" after the laying of the body in the family vault. The black she wore made her pale skin shimmer. Despite her proper bun tied up at her neck, she was making Ietsy melt like fat in the sun. He would have followed her like a puppy dog forever if Arthur hadn't elbowed him in the ribs.

The thinning group of friends talked a little on their way to where the cars were parked. No one had heard from Jeannie. Arthur and Néness already knew their fates. The former was going back to the French high school. His parents had questioned him at length, but he was a lucky bastard and got the love part of tough love. The latter was staying at Sintème like nothing had happened. He even got to keep his scholarship. In the nude chaos that had followed their experiments, no one had noticed his absence from class. Arthur, the only one in any state to answer the questions they'd been subject to in the rector's office—in between uncontrollable fits of laughter—hadn't mentioned him. So Néness had just kept sleeping under the pines until cold rain woke him up. He hadn't returned home until nightfall. The next day at school, he first heard the rumors in the courtyard, then in the auditorium the official version about the group's misconduct, then the final disciplinary action directly after. The other students were unnerved: drugs at Sintème, it was simply unthinkable for most of them. When Took, the class wiseass, tried to rechristen the courtyard the "Garden of Eden," he and Néness were the only two who'd laughed. Everyone else had glared daggers at them.

It was the last time that Ietsy Razak saw his friends for a long while. The next day, after his father made him take a handful of red dirt from near the ancestral tomb, he put Ietsy on a plane to a boarding school beyond the seas, run this time by Benedictine monks, on the banks of a river that disappeared underground.

A long time ago, even before the era of Gola, at the very beginning, it is said a man accidentally fell from the sky. His name was Ietsy. Some of the poets sing that he tumbled down as he beheld the beauty of this land, trusted by the sea. As he had fainted, Breath dispatched the rainbow to go down and revive him. He was the first. The first to swoon at the sight of this island—it was already solid back then, and enchanted—and, once he'd come to again, the first to fall for it. There was no one on the island besides him. He was quite happy to be there, although he felt a little alone.

He went to where the colored band of light landed, over and over again, to see if there were any travelers, one woman, or even one man who would come down. He'd sent messages lauding the island and its abundance of everything, but no one came to live with him or visit him. In his solitude, he considered exploring somewhere else. But just for an instant, for he loved the island so much that the thought of leaving it seemed, after his fall, a letdown. "Better to bury myself here!" he said, according to the Talily, the ancestral memories.

So he stayed to ramble the rocky highlands, shaded valleys, and craggy bluffs, following rivers from lake to lake. His walks were beautiful but lonely. As he rested, on a mountaintop, beside a river, or in the shade of a ficus, he sculpted statues in the image of himself and the women of his dreams.

Every time that Breath dropped in without travelers or messages for him, she saw his disappointment and distress. Still, Ietsy persevered in wanting to stay. She offered to help him again. She was not yet the old woman we know her as. Breath could not have children but found Ietsy's breathless statues beautiful enough to fill them with her breath of life. If, and only if, Ietsy would agree to be a father to them. Of course, this condition was the exact opposite of everything Ietsy had dreamed of. But he needed company. He agreed. Breath breathed into the statues, and they became alive. Thus, the only unearthly part of the island's first people was their breath, their soul. That's what makes humans human, they say—before, we were just wooden statues!

Ietsy, enticed by some of his dreams made flesh, obviously did not keep his word and was tempted to seduce first one, then more of his progeny. As this generally took place at night and Breath had the whole sky at her window, she caught wind of it and swore she would take back her breath from this small, incestuous world. She returned, jealous and vindictive, but couldn't distinguish the wheat from the chaff, as they would later say. The men created in Ietsy's image and the women embodying his dreams, the children all looked alike. Vexed, Breath took back her breaths arbitrarily, at random. And thus did Ietsy's children know death, soon after receiving their name: Vazimbas, or Children of the Broken Vow.

Since then, Vazimbas give their lives to Breath but return their bodies to Ietsy's land. In this country, where people take such pride in their origins, bastards have had the same face as everyone else from the very beginning, and essentially the same destiny; that is to say, every person has their own—the so-called purity of origins has no influence on it at all.

Ietsy lived 391 years before fate caught him. Tears flowed in fountains, for the Vazimbas cherished him. As one, they drew beside the lifeless body. Respecting Ietsy's wishes, they buried him under the ground and named the place Tsievonana, The-Place-Where-No-One-Sneezes. They came from all the places Ietsy had left them when he had sculpted them. They all came, for Ietsy had loved them all and they all recognized him as the originator of their days.

From then on something was missing for those cast in his image, as if a lamba had been lost in a gust of wind on a stormy day. Thus, they knew cold, sneezing. In his memory we exclaim *"IETSY!"* when we sneeze. Breath also understood the absence and eased her punishment.

31

However, death continued its work, and life its course. Sloping gently, sometimes steeper, jagged, and uneven, strewn with traps, but leaving like the wellspring, alone, creek, flowing, swirling stream then river, even drying out, rarely climbing, often, yes, gently sloping down to the sea. And, as they say, *Angano angano, arira arira*, a legend is a legend, the truth is another, it is not I who lie but those who transmitted it to me.

So it was written in gold embossed letters in the copy of the Talily that Ietsy Razak's father had given him when he left the Land of the Ancestors. He'd also given him two Bibles, one Protestant in Malagasy, the other Catholic in French. Ietsy never took those out of his bags. He'd learned very quickly that these people from beyond the seas gave him weird looks when he talked about religion. So, he avoided it. Over there, spiritual questions broke off at his fairly un-Catholic name. In the Benedictine school, they sometimes called him "Che" for short, even though most of his classmates—sons and daughters of the bourgeoisie, even some aristocrats—knew nothing of the revolutionary's feats. It wasn't worth it to talk to them about the Talily and its enchantments. They whispered enough among themselves when they noticed Ietsy writing and receiving letters in a strange language.

His father had given him the Great Ancestor's name, maybe to ensure his protection or ward off evil, I don't know. He'd actually gotten off to a bad start. His mother, as she threw him into the river of life, left via the East, the shore of origins and death. And not like in the myth of Ibonia, where the child symbolically kills the laboring woman as they come into the world, only to resuscitate the mother later: she went away for real.

This caused the boy some angst, and granted him some freedoms—there were benefits too. No one would insult his maternal side, for it was universally sensitive. If by chance someone was unaware of the ancestral status of the one who'd given birth to him and called him a son of a whore, there were always plenty of others around to teach them what blasphemy had been uttered. Most of the time, Ietsy feigned magnanimity and was thus able to get anything he wanted from the poor soul—guilt, and the fear of retribution from dead saints, would leave them at the mercy of the motherless child. Sometimes, he would beat them up, beat them hard, to teach them to be quiet, beat them up until the boiling tears he refused to let out were stilled.

When he was older, his story moved some girls to pity and a surge of tenderness, which he could always transform into something just as tender as a mother's loving caresses—although far from as chaste. He didn't play around with telling his woeful story every time. However, by dint of being a plaything to these women, his aunts, his housekeeper, his father's secretaries, all the female friends of the family, especially those with kindly dispositions who would have liked to become a good stepmother for him and take his mother's place in the heart of Mr. Razak—who had never actually considered himself absolved of his first promise of loyalty—he could play his hand very well with them.

His friends envied him and interrogated him. He prided himself on his reassuring way with girls. Sometimes he'd act indifferent, which was apparently attractive, but to be clear, he didn't go too far with the show. He'd always had plenty of little loves, as Charlie called them. When one let out a swooning call of his name, he never teased her by asking if she'd come down with a cold. But girls were like anything else: when you went out with one, the rest were never far off. Mediocre minds would point out his status—the only kid in a rich old family—but frankly, who in that milieu wasn't an heir to something? Cynical minds would reason that eligible young women would be far less afraid of a ghostly mother-in-law than a flesh-and-blood shrew who would stick her nose in every aspect of the young couple's lives. In any case, he would have preferred that people pay attention to his personal charms. He was tall—a rare thing in Imerina, these highlands under the skies—with light skin, very popular around these parts, and shiny, black, straight hair above an intelligent forehead and symmetrical yet sensual face. But truth be told, he didn't understand how it worked, either. More specifically, it never worked when he wanted it to. People envied him for his abundant advantages, but not for anything he'd actually done.

Not that he was spurning his luck, but he wanted to have the choice. He'd always been chosen. Even though he could avoid the girls he didn't like, he hadn't really been able to get close to his heart's true love. He was incapable of taking action to win someone over. His hands got clammy, legs shaky, lips dry. And if by chance his most secret wishes were fulfilled, his life drained from him, his will shattered by fear. As if the simple fact of wanting to love, to live, ran the risk of killing the one he loved, or himself.

This morbid anxiety meant that he was forced to hate the girls he desired most. He would have to find the fault that they generally tried to keep hidden, a weak forehead hiding behind bangs, an eye that wandered ever so slightly, bony knees, unshapely toes, imperfections that let him love without fear. And thus he went, from conquest to conquest, without any real victory, except for one. Obviously I don't mean his wife, Lea-Nour: she was on a different level altogether; she was destined for him. His father's words of the union of earth and water at their wedding had been fitting ones. But I'm moving too fast. For the moment, the field is still unsown.

Ietsy was welcomed in France by his father's elder, only brother. Uncle Jean had married a French woman. Aunt Christiane, who wasn't able to have children, had treasured baby Ietsy. She'd moved almost permanently to Anosisoa to take care of him. Yes, of course there was enough room in Anosisoa for several families. Yes, of course Uncle Jean and his wife had a place in Anosisoa. However, gradually, the bond that the woman was creating with the child eclipsed the relationship between the two brothers. Christiane's foreign origins, even though her family had been on the island for a long time, and even more so the fact that she couldn't give Jean an heir, had already pushed them away from Anosisoa once. What was more, the whole story of the Razak brothers with the Lamothe girl offended some people's delicate sensibilities at the dawn of independence and was thwarting the grandfather's political ambitions. So, they left for Paris before Ietsy turned three years old.

Ietsy had no memory of all that. He liked his relatives from beyond the seas. When they'd come back to the country for important family events, turnings of the dead, weddings, burials, his circumcision, they'd always brought him lots of presents. But he didn't remember his aunt stretching out her maternal arms to give him a secure infancy.

As she told him about that not-so-long-ago past in their Parisian apartment, she dissolved into tears. Ietsy was just fifteen and didn't know what to do with his gangly body when faced with a crying woman. She would probably make a decent mom, he guessed, unable to get himself out of the overstuffed armchair.

Fortunately, Uncle Jean was there. He looked like his brother, but younger despite his age, perhaps because he was clean-shaven and wore his hair long, tied back with a strip of leather. He finished serving the lemongrass-infused tea and sat next to her on the couch, taking her in his arms.

"There were so many rumors in your family back then," his aunt continued, reaching for her husband's hand. "All unfounded. Nothing happened between your father and me. I only wanted to fill in for your mother . . . but you're not my son!"

Her frail body shook with gentle sobs. Then she pulled herself together and talked to him about Marlène. It was one of the few times that had happened in Ietsy's short life. There were plenty of pictures of his mother all around Anosisoa: in the sitting room and in his father's office, the ones from their engagement and wedding in the hall with a spread of other photographs as old as the trade itself, large portraits of her by herself in the library, probably taken those same two days, and then the one in Ietsy's room in her normal clothes, which was also in the locket his father had solemnly given him for his birthday one year. Despite noticeable effort, his father had never been able to say more than a few sentences about her in front of him, except in a few exceptional circumstances. Plus silence was the norm in their relationship, anyway.

The first time he'd been told about his mother was when they were bringing the deceased new lambamenas. Ietsy was maybe eight or nine. There were two colorfully dressed operetta troupes, *mpihira gasy*, taking turns outdoing one another as they danced and acted out scenes from folklore; they'd sacrificed a black zebu with a white spot on its forehead. Someone had brought a grand piano, glossy and black before the dull red dust of the tomb, which some of the many family members played from time to time. A master flutist accompanied them, wearing the traditional white toga and straw hat. They had opened the heavy stone door and brought out the venerated relics. His maternal grandfather had told him that his mother was those pieces of bone, those clumps of hair that had kept growing, those bits of earth writhing around in the mat that people were carrying and passing hand to hand as they danced and yelled, and that she was watching over him. The first turning of the bones, his mother's father explained, marked a new passage, a kind of consecration—they went from simply being deceased relatives to becoming ancestral protectors.

At the end of the afternoon, once everything had been carefully rewrapped in more than twenty shrouds of wild silks, the famous lambamenas, and returned to its place, Ietsy's grandfather took the child to see the interior of the stone house. He showed him the ledges, lining the walls like bookshelves, where his mother, his grandmother, his maternal great-grandparents, and other more distant forebears rested.

Ietsy hadn't yet understood why his mother was there, in Ambatofotsy, far from their home, while he and his father would go to the vault in Anosisoa after their deaths. But he had an excellent memory of the terrible nightmares he'd had after returning from his visit to the ancestors, despite calling on his favorite dreams when he closed his eyes.

Eyes open or closed, he often pictured scenarios that showed him in the best light. A prized one was him driving a blue Porsche with one of his father's friend's prettiest daughters: Lea-Nour. This time, he was doing the Easter rally with her, Tana–Ampefy–Antsirabe. It usually started off well, they'd get the best qualifying time on the hilly Ankatso–Ambohidempona course, but that night, once he was fully asleep, the Porsche headed straight for the tomb, and he ended up alone inside the stone with slender mounds of clay that claimed to be his relatives, like his mother. He screamed and woke up all of Anosisoa. His father had an herbal tea brought to him, left a light on, told him to read, but nothing worked—every time he fell asleep, he ended up again and again surrounded by the remains of his forebears.

He spent that night in the bed of his father, who, once his son was sleeping calmly, took the divan next to it. Upon waking, Ietsy was both disconcerted by and grateful for it.

These memories made him shiver again all those years later in his aunt and uncle's apartment. Sharing them, however, brought some warmth.

"I remember that exhumation very well," Aunt Christiane said. "It was the most beautiful ceremony I'd ever attended—not as lavish as Anosisoa, but more . . . I don't know how to explain it, more elegant? I bet it's your mother's artistic side!"

"But why wasn't she buried in Anosisoa?"

"The proverb says, 'In life, we live in the same house; in death, we will remain in the same tomb,'" Uncle Jean said. "However, in our family, ever since our forebears settled in Anosisoa, the tomb has been reserved for the males. According to lore, there were some fussy in-laws who had disapproved of the fact that Anosisoa was only one head above the water level—a tomb that low was not worthy of their clan, and they would not allow their daughter, your great-great-grandmother, to join our side. The children's will eventually triumphed over the parents' huffiness—they were able to marry, but under the express condition that the daughter's body come back to her family's tomb on a mountaintop, as it should be. Our patriarch, to conceal his wounded pride, decided that from that moment on, Anosisoa would never allow daughters-in-law a place in the cold house."

Ietsy was intrigued. "So, will you two also be separated at death?"

"We've made arrangements to stay by each other's side, here in a plot at Père Lachaise," Uncle Jean said, laughing.

"My own uncle will not be buried in the Land of the Ancestors?"

Ietsy's stomach turned at the idea, his inner Malagasy soul rising up beneath the French words. Foreign lands, even with such close relatives, certainly held many surprises, and shocks. But he could not go so far as to judge his uncle; rather, he merely expressed his regret that custom would prevent him from ever being close to his mother.

"Don't think like that, my boy," his uncle consoled him. "No matter where her body lies, your mother is always with you!"

"No matter where you are!" Aunt Christiane reassured him, taking several photo albums out from a shelf beneath the coffee table.

"Before she became your guardian angel, Marlène was a sweet woman who loved life," she said, showing Ietsy photographs taken before his birth and during his infancy. "She had a gift for music, and dexterous fingers she used to win over your father. That grand piano at the exhumation ceremony, that was hers, a gift from your father. After she died, your father couldn't stand to hear even one note, so he got rid of it. The piano wound up with one of your aunts."

"And I never got any musical education," Ietsy interrupted as he stopped at a series of photos of him as a baby in his aunt Christiane's arms—he seemed to be squealing and trying to grab her nose.

"Yes, you did." Uncle Jean smiled. "With your mother's sister, the one who'd taken the piano. You didn't want to go, your father never understood why."

"He probably didn't mind!"

"Probably not."

"Marlène and I had been friends before marrying into the same family," his aunt continued. "Her arrival in Anosisoa was quite the breath of fresh air. Even your grandfather was mollified by her music and sweet disposition. She would have loved to see the world. She was happy with your father, although she understood that to marry him was to marry the land as well: the end of her dream to travel. It wasn't so easy to cross the ocean back then. When she was pregnant with you, you moved a lot. She would rub her belly and say that you'd travel the whole world someday."

Ietsy's mouth hung open. He didn't feel like crying anymore.

They talked again about the events that had led his father to send him to France. Ietsy hung his head, listened, but he felt like their reprimands didn't affect him, wouldn't affect him anymore. Experimenting with dreams and parallel lives hadn't ever tempted him that much—or at least less than the grown-ups around him wanted to believe. His aunt had shed some light on a shadowy part of his life. It didn't make up for his loss, of course. But he somehow understood that something in him had found an answer. Two days later, on the way to his dormitory in the nearby suburb of Bièvres, he promised them, before they asked, as if in gratitude for their warm welcome, that he would never touch drugs again.

He felt at ease with Jean and Christiane, able to have open conversations with them. But regardless, he did not say a word to them about the awkwardness he'd felt coming from the airport the first morning he'd arrived. He'd seen a whole spread of photos of scantily clad women and obscene words in the large tunnels they'd walked through. At Sintème, imported magazines with similar images were sometimes passed feverishly around underneath the boys' tables during their evening study period. Ietsy's imagination would get carried away thumbing through the pages, and often his entire groin hardened and hurt for a long time after the crumpled magazine had returned to its hiding place, usually stuck underneath its owner's shirt. The fire that burned inside of him then was more intense than what he'd felt merely seeing a naked Jeannie. Although he'd never considered applying what the Jesuits taught in their sex ed classes, as they especially recommended to calm one's mind with ice water if tormented by temptations, he had inherited, in addition to his highlander modesty, a notion of sex based on puritanical teachings and bundling up. So, when he saw, plastered on the side of a newspaper kiosk just beside their car stopped at a red light, a larger-than-life naked woman saying to contact her via Minitel, he didn't dare look at his uncle sitting behind the wheel, for fear that he'd seen it too.

Despite first impressions, Ietsy wasn't completely unfamiliar with this place his father had sent him to beyond the seas. Although he'd never set foot there before, he'd become very familiar with the language. The island's prominent families had adopted the colonists' language along with their religion, although not going so far as to leave Malagasy behind. French was used both to communicate with foreigners and between Malagasies sometimes to exclude those who hadn't mastered it—and vice versa.

Ietsy's culture was both Malagasy and French, with emphasis on writing in the latter. Printed texts, from the literary classics to weekly magazines, defined the imaginary France of his childhood and obviously impeded his ability to grasp the real one. Seeing as how they'd only socialized with high-society people in Antananarivo and sometimes received princesses at home in Anosisoa, he expected to meet Stéphanie of Monaco in the City of Lights, since the magazines—the ones that lay around the lobbies of Razak businesses—said she spent lots of time there. He never saw her outside the normal glossy pages. He of course never spoke of his disappointment until much later, when he could laugh about it, although he had surprised himself by defending the intrepid princess to some of the snobs from the Bièvres boarding school at a rally, the first and last he was invited to. Beyond that, he only dimly picked up on the distance between his imagination and reality, just like the distance between what he thought of himself and what others thought of the foreign student, although his close friends forgot about his origins and the color of his skin, because fundamentally, he was just like them.

This time, he got up and slipped noiselessly out the back.

Anosisoa, like the other islands in the Antananarivo basin—backfilled, more and more gray, less and less green, in the middle of the granite string of sacred mountains—barely deserved to be called an island anymore. It was separated from the rice fields by a thick, solid wall of red earth; rice still grew in some of the fields, but others were filled in with suburbs and the industrial zone spreading north of the city. The sole entrance was a sturdy iron bridge, its thick joists rattling against each other as they expanded and contracted over time, groaning under passing wheels depending on the vehicle's weight. Outbuildings for rice, sheds for agricultural equipment, a silo, and a treatment plant all sat on the fringes and brought it to life during the day.

Through a small forest of acacias and fig trees, the residence came into view. Three buildings of different sizes made a U shape, with a royal sycamore dominating the center, as it should, shading old beds of rosebushes and poinsettias on a stretch of unruly lawn.

In one wing, former stables had become a garage, with a second floor where the staff lived, three families plus the housekeeper and the latest driver, both unmarried, the first by vocation and the second by virtue of youth. Across the way and set slightly farther back, a two-story wooden house had once held offices, which were now in the city, for Mr. Razak had remodeled them into comfortable apartments for himself and his own father when his first granddaughter came along.

Now, the main building, where Ietsy was coming out from, was the epitome of a Central Highlands house, three times larger than average, with exposed brick, wood reinforcements, and a slate roof. Its imposing size was due as much to the initial builders' ambitions as their successors' desires to adapt it to new needs, like rooms for leisure. In the front, then, a glass wall framed the former parlor, now divided into a living room and a library, while at the back, two lean-tos framed the veranda, one doubling the size of the serving pantry and kitchen, the other a playroom for the children, used mostly by the adults to store anything and everything, since the kids generally preferred to lord over the attic lofts.

The whole ensemble restricted access to the highest point on the Enchanted Island, barely higher than the rest: the location of the tomb.

After lighting a cigarette under the veranda, Ietsy bypassed the drive lined with jacarandas; walked around the pool, an example of the significant progress Lea-Nour had brought to the old residence; and went down the little path that wound through the slumbering garden, more perfumed on that side with its jasmine trees, francisceas, and tall clumps of lemongrass, toward a pond that was hidden from view by a curtain of papyrus. And as he strolled around it, he realized that it no longer reflected even the moon, because of the hyacinths that had taken over the surface and spared only a few last patches of resistant water lilies.

The pond had been dug at the same time as the Andriamasinavalona dikes were constructed to tame the Ikopa River that wrapped itself around Antananarivo, four centuries ago, when the Betsimitatatra rice fields were being wrested from the marshes by unending labor that brought the entire population of Imerina together, after they'd driven away the former masters of the land, the Vazimban-drano.

For the Children of the Broken Vow, the original people of the great island—whether they be those of the coasts, Vazimban-driaka; of the forests, Vazimban'ala; of the mountains, Vazimbam-bohitra; or of the waters, Vazimban-drano, and later of the savannas, Vazimban-tanety, established where the great Ietsy had sculpted their ancestors—were all forever betrayed by those who came after belatedly answering the Great Ancestor's call, more greedy and having made no vows, to seize the land of the Vazimbas. These others, unable to exterminate the natives—who grew like weeds, or rather like sacred wood—endeavored to forge alliances with Ietsy's children. Alliances often later forgotten, if not renounced entirely, but believed necessary to inherit their virtues and uncover their secrets, which were said to contain, in addition to the key to the island's riches, the mysteries of life, of first breath. And the Vazimbas, in accordance with Ietsy's wishes, assimilated and absorbed each new wave of arrivals, trying to release them from their fantastical quests by opening their bastard hearts to them. But love is a difficult thing to understand for those who have not been bathed in it from birth. Feelings of exclusion and disappointment were often accompanied by violence, which ate away at the flesh of land and children, burying still deeper what always could have been within reach.

The newcomers split into two camps: those who thought they understood Ietsy's children and those who gave up on that. All of them, though, once they felt an attachment to the land, ended up in the melting pot. Thus the first immigrants came, Gola the Magnificent and his companions from beyond the seas, from the northeast, searching for Ietsy's treasure.

In Tsievonana, as the Talily tells it, one of Ietsy's daughters stayed to guard his tomb, with the face of Ietsy's final dream. Her name was Ratiakolalaina, The-One-You'd-Like-to-Love, given that name by her father because he was already counting his days when she was born. He spent his old age doting on her and delighting her with little animals he molded with his still-dexterous hands, just before his final moments. Any joy he gave her, she returned to him a hundredfold when her lips parted to smile. At ten years old, she was already so beautiful that the sun went into heat on the hill every time she went outside. For a while, there were no more nights and days. In the confusion, Ietsy withdrew further from mankind, achieved serenity after his disjointed life. Despite his self-imposed solitude, he saw Ratiakolalaina several times in dreams, and took seven years to die.

When breath left Ietsy, his beloved daughter peacefully awoke in her bed and knew that her father had died. She left her hut and went to the place from where Ietsy's soul had departed. The sun escorted her through her journey and tried to dry her tears. The Vazimbas, who were joining her one by one to kneel before Ietsy's cold body, found her lying prostrate before a small pool made from her tears. She did not move when they put him under this earth, respecting the patriarch's wishes. It was as if she did not see them at all during the entire ceremony. At the end, they sat next to her for a time to share her grief. Some of them enlarged the pool with their own tears. Others, who could not, set down gold or silver. When they departed, they left, in addition to Ratiakolalaina, appointed guardian of the tomb, a mountain of gold and silver and a lake as deep as a good man's eye. After a time equal to seven more years, as Ratiakolalaina's sorrow would not ebb and the sun, weary, began again to circle the earth, the lake swelled and engulfed the tomb and its guardian. But instead of drowning her, the lake gave life to its wellspring. With love beyond measure, she continued to care for her father's tomb under the water and was more beautiful than ever. She also had children, only girls, each as beautiful as she. As if Ietsy had finally fulfilled his dreams, safe from Breath's anger in the watery world.

The Zazavavindranos, these Daughters-of-the-Water, still haunt the banks of our lily pad ponds, some rivers. Deep in our hearts. Since, as they say, the beauty of their souls shines forth in their bodies, they show themselves only to righteous young men. They can accept the men's marriage proposals, give them children, riches, longevity, if only the chosen ones maintain a pure heart. If not, they dive into the nearest body of water and disappear forever. Likewise if their complex taboos are violated. According to the stories, you must never divulge where these mermaids came from. We know that Ranour, one of the most well-known Zazavavindranos, made her husband promise to avoid all contact with salt. He was not even allowed to utter the word. But some prohibitions are so subtle that wicked minds see them as mere excuses for the watergirls to return to their natural element. If on the off chance, within life's ebb and flow, you should come across one of them, she pulls you from your solitude, bathes you in a perfume of eternity in the space of a breath, and dries you with a towel even more quickly. Then everything returns to the way it was before. The wind breathes, blows the rain clouds away, and the dust remains dust.

Later, after the first Ietsy and also farther, beyond the seas, in the land of dawn, the Talily says, Gola had been training since his initiation to hold his breath. He hoped to make his bathing last longer. He was so dedicated to his breath-holding that he did not notice the water filling in around him until much too late. But as he was not content with it, he did not even get wet. He could go out in the rain, in storms (he was a sailor), under cascading waterfalls—water evaded him. At thirty years old, Gola was still dry. He was nicknamed Andriatsilena, or The-Lord-Who-Never-Gets-Wet. Yet his greatest desire was to bathe, even for an instant, in the ecstasy of love. Even only for an instant, for as his age increased, he was much less concerned with the duration, and he secretly had hope.

One fine day, Gola found a sarimanok on the beach with a broken wing. The seabird seemed exhausted from a long journey. Yet beneath its feathers, Gola found only a trace of an old wound. The bones in its left wing were a little shorter but, to his touch, seemed to have healed. As Gola stroked the sarimanok's down, he was surprised to find a few drops of water on his hand. The crystalline beads tickled as they slipped down his fingers, opening his pores to an unknown yet pleasant sensation. He brought a drop to his mouth and felt what flowers experience as they open their petals to the morning dew. Fascinated, Gola, who'd never been wet before, rushed to ask the bird where it had come from.

The sarimanok told him that in its last migration, its wing wounded, the trade winds had carried it farther south than in previous journeys. It had run aground on a vast land. Exhausted, convinced its final hour had come, the sarimanok looked for a noble place for its passage into the world of shadows. With a final effort, it flew above blue mountains and, within a valley of golden slopes, found a pool so blue that light itself came to gaze at its own reflection. It alighted a little off to the side and serenely began its mortuary song. Two young women, each as beautiful as the other, came from the water and drew near. The sarimanok thought they were messengers of death and had no fear. The Daughters-of-the-Water brought the bird near the pool, washed it, and cared for it. The water restored it, and, that very evening with the two beautiful caregivers, its wound already scarred, it sang melodies that were much less funereal. The sarimanok remained there for several seasons. Yet it had promised itself to return to the land of dawn to pass down to others' ears what had been its joy.

As you can imagine, the words sown by the sarimanok sprouted into an idea, which in Gola's mind blossomed easily into a grand plan. Gola dreamed of bathing in that extraordinary pool—which was of course the pool of Ratiakolalaina's tears—which would soak him down to his core, he was sure of it, yes, even his heart, dried up by so many arid years.

And so Gola made preparations for the great crossing. First, he had to persuade his people to come with him. Gola extolled the faraway island with somewhat different words than the sarimanok. Yes, he told them the story about the bird with the broken left wing and the famed drops under its down. He stressed the size of the gold mountain. But even with a few dreamers among his friends who would follow him for any folly, many of them wanted more-convincing arguments before rallying behind this movement started by the legend of The-Lord-Who-Never-Gets-Wet in search of water to wet his skin. Gola said to those mistrustful people who didn't know much: "Over there lies the future!" But they weren't sure what that was and asked the oracle for an explanation. The island was so far away that the prophet they consulted, having already decided to help Gola, took a risk and said, "Over there, in every village, you will be honored both during and well after your lifetime!"

"But," protested the skeptics, "what exactly is the future?"

The holy man simply said, "No one gets over it."

That seemed true. They, too, made preparations for the great crossing.

For the trade winds to push them straight to the wide future, or Madagasikara, they built boats in the image of the wounded sarimanok: small crafts of two joined hulls with a smaller left wing. The hulls were hollowed out from tree trunks, with boards on the edges to lengthen them. Woven palms joined them together. From felling the first tree trunk to applying the final coat of resin to seal the boats, they worked five months and seventeen days. Each prow and stern were set with sculpted panels, the fore ones peering into the future and the aft spanning the past. They did not bless the boats, for the sacred water was the water they would cross. After a three-day fast and a fire purification ceremony, they climbed on board. Seven times seven of the great outriggers held two or three families and the year's harvest of rice, obviously, and feasts of fowl and coconuts, as the length of the journey was unknown. They hoisted their single square sails, white or multicolored, on the first moon after the equinox of the 397th wind season before the era of Gola. Bound south-southwest, for the Cape of the Broken Wing. The *Sarimanok*, Gola's aerocraft, black and gold, sailed at the head over the surface of the waters. He was dreaming of feeling the water, and beside him, Ietsy Razak's ancestors were thinking of the mountain of gold and silver.

What happened could only come to pass after heavy costs paid and several adventures, both warlike and romantic. After completing the crossing by walking on giant water lilies, Gola found bliss in the arms of Nour, a daughter of the seventeenth generation of Vazimbas after Ietsy's death. From the moment the newcomers arrived on the eastern coast, the Vazimbas' gifts of welcome repaid their investments a hundredfold. Ietsy's children on the east of the island and Gola's companions settled their blood pact and bred together.

Alas, Gola did not find the sacred lake, and the searches for the mountain of gold and silver turned up nothing. Did he have faith when Nour told him that the place lay deep in his heart? Nour, who became Ranour the Holy, who threw herself into a crocodile-infested river rather than hear her sailor husband complain of his lack of salt.

At first, the People of Gola increased in number, pressed forward over the lands and forests, and reached the Central Highlands. A few centuries after the first landing, a thousand warriors, Ietsy Razak's ancestors among them, conquered Analamanga, The-Blue-Forest-Mountain, the most beautiful of the twelve sacred hills, jewels set in sparkling waters, and from then on called it Antananarivo, or The-City-of-Thousands.

Then they had to tame the Ikopa River, which was flooding the Antananarivo basin, and first and foremost their former masters, so that we would never again want for rice. It was the battle of the *horaka*, or wet war, a battle only in name against the natives of the swamps, the Vazimban-drano, who fled far away from the flying staffs of iron, as pacifist as their cousins met before. The great dike construction project and draining of the marshes could begin, which would engrave King Andriamasinavalona's name in history.

Ietsy Razak's forebears, who'd been behind the idea, wanted to commemorate the occasion by establishing their residence on the largest of the islets, Anosisoa. They of course kept a house near the Rova on the royal hill, but as the generations passed, they slowly moved out. They were deemed insane to abandon the high hills for Amboniloha, those substandard lands infested with mosquitoes and liable to flood every rainy season, and emerging barely a head above the level of the water the rest of the year. In the beginning, they lived close to the king, going there only to oversee the construction and harvests. Then, the dikes were reinforced, the rice fields expanded, and the Vazimbas pushed ever farther west or assimilated, so they were able to move there permanently, only going back up to the city for special occasions. They even built a tomb there.

Once drained, the swamps provided good soil for rice and became a reliable supply for the city as it developed around the Rova, keeping the specter of scarcity at bay when uncertain times came and resources from the faraway countryside didn't arrive. In Ietsy's grandfather's time, colonists occupied the blessed city in the hills, and it was the members of the court, then whatever was left of it, who bent over backward to get to Anosisoa for festivals. Later, the rice fields between there and the city slowly started being filled in. The Razaks stingily granted a small parcel of them to the serfs freed by the French administration but kept the rest lying fallow until the independence government opportunely decreed it an industrial zone.

There was always plenty of water in Anosisoa, although it rained less than at higher elevations. Winters were pleasant there. And his forebears had proven prescient about mosquito-transmitted malaria as well. Having noticed that pipistrelle bats consumed thousands of insects in a single night, they planted sycamores and fig trees with large leafy branches, where the odd flying creatures liked to hang upside down to prepare for their insect hunts. No longer fearing the humidity or mosquitoes, they even kept the pond.

The Anosisoa pond was clearly not Ratiakolalaina's pool. But it was a symbol of renouncing the Great Ancestor's mythical search for treasure and setting down roots in the soil, the land. Ietsy Razak had swum there as a child in the summer. He was disappointed that his children didn't care to discover the feeling of pleasure tinged with uncertainty when slipping into the pond, feet squelching into silky warm mud, brushing curious or startled fish. Like Lea-Nour, who'd had the swimming pool installed, their children preferred its tiled bottom and clear water to the mysteries of the pond that burst with life.

He walked around it again as he smoked another cigarette. His watch showed just after one o'clock. He wasn't tired at all. For the past week he hadn't been sleeping. It was unsettling. The first night, he hadn't gotten up and instead waited for the dawn with his eyes bulging into the dark. Ditto the second. The third, he slipped outside to take a walk, hoping to fall back asleep after a breath of fresh air. It didn't work. His eyes obstinately open, he waited for any sign of his youngest, who always woke up first, to give himself a reason to get up. The following night, he was planning on reading. But he'd woken his wife up with an unfortunately abrupt movement—he'd gotten the sheets caught underneath himself and only realized it when rolling over to pick up his book—and got such a dressing-down that he didn't dare move or turn on the light again. So he set himself up in a separate room with a stack of books. But for all that work, he didn't read, persisting in the search for sleep, or the reason for his futile quest.

I'm not even worried about the future, he reasoned, standing perplexed by the pond.

He told himself that the journey to the end of the night would once again be long. The words popped out of his insomniac mind like air bubbles from an aquatic plant on the water's surface.

THE SHADOW OF BABYLON

At another time in his life during which he didn't sleep much, the nighttime hours trickled away in smoke-filled, slightly drunken debates on life, art, the autonomy of books, the character of authors, on Céline, Gombrowicz, and the like. But he recovered from those crazy nights the very next day. He crawled out of his bed in late morning, usually without a hangover. He recovered quickly, as they say. He was a student. Not a literature student, for as it was established upon his departure from the Land of the Ancestors three years before taking the Bac, it was law school for him. Still, most of the time, he read something other than his law books. Perhaps that hunger came from his friend Charlie, his aunt Christiane's influence, or boredom at the Bièvres boarding school.

He struck up a friendship with Boris, another aficionado of literature, with whom he lived in a huge apartment in Versailles during his five years of law school (more specifically, they'd crashed at Boris's father's place, the father having left his residence behind for the Côte d'Azur—it was too near to the capital). They discussed and exchanged books, CDs, and girls, or more often their impressions of that raw material, all night long, all the while blithely plundering the vintage reserves of Eugène K., Boris's father.

Boris, like Ietsy, had lost his mother. He'd known her, of course, had lived with her for a little while, but more importantly, when he was eleven years old, had watched her die after a long and painful battle with cancer. From his suffering, which had seemed endless back then, he'd developed a hatred for everyone who seemed not to feel the same, especially for his older sisters; they'd already left home when the tragedy struck and had fallen instantly on their mother's jewelry box after the burial. He was angry with his father, too, who hadn't been able to prevent the pillaging, as he called it. He snarled awful things at them, sparing neither their egos nor their ears. The unplanned yet unruly child was dropped off with the Benedictines. There, his pain changed at the same time as his voice to become youthful disdain for all things ephemeral, particularly the people attached to such things. Céline's *Journey* was his Bible, and he converted Ietsy.

For Ietsy, emerging from the cocoon of Bièvres, the Versailles era was when he attended the school of life, without anyone to intercede in any of his relationships. He felt kinship. He endured violence, humiliations, sometimes even fear in a country where he hadn't expected to feel like a foreigner. Paradoxically, because he'd never really become a part of it, he hadn't adopted the hatred of other young people whom he met on public transit or in shopping malls, drawn to him because of the color of his skin but who didn't have a faraway place to hang their hopes like he did. He felt love, passion that knows no law, and its violent cruelty. At the end of his fourth year at law school, with no particular mishaps or brilliant results, he had his Andriba.

The Andriba was a mountain on the western edge of the Central Highlands. On its slopes in 1895, the queen's army scattered and fled in terror before the explosion of melanite shells from the vanguard of the French army that had come to conquer Madagascar for the second time. Although the overall forces of both sides were unequal and the kingdom would have had to surrender sooner or later to a greater power, Andriba, according to his great-grandfather who had been there with his own father, one of the queen's officers, symbolized above all defeat without a fight, the worst kind, leaving the wounds open to questions and preventing healthy predictions about the future. His forefather had warned him about it, and still Ietsy fell.

He met Ninon during one of those soirées he was so fond of with his rejected rally friends, as summer was stealthily approaching. After his first car rally in his final year at Bièvres, he'd realized very quickly that regular ralliers were too infatuated with themselves; they didn't know how to have fun, listened to crappy music, and wasted their time making awkward appearances at parties and having politically correct conversations, which, given his origins, never could have included him anyway. The core group in Versailles had formed a loose cluster of party animals, international and also native French students, who loved the night and "real" music. They got together all the time, on the Right Bank below the Louvre or the Left Bank under the Pont Neuf, or sometimes overlooking the river on the Pont des Arts, which they liked less because it was too crowded, or in the garden at the tip of Île Saint-Louis, which they had to hop the fence to get to. They would spend the beginning or end of an evening out there, sometimes the whole night if certain arrangements were made, a bar or picnic, or themed parties, a simple costume, sometimes just a color to wear or an attitude to adopt, then of course invitations for the most beautiful girls, the hottest ones, lured by something different, who'd in turn lure good musicians who'd lure more girls, and so on. Sometimes five, six, ten, even twenty or more would get together, surrounded by city lights reflected on the water's surface.

One May night, cross-dressing, silk stockings over hairy legs, garter belts, fake boobs, makeup, wigs for some, a large lacy scarf with fake violets on Ietsy's head, they put on a scene from *La Cage aux Folles* to celebrate a good friend's birthday and distract her from the next day's exams. The masquerade ball drew a crowd, and the cake meant for seven—an intimate gathering—was cut into sixteenths.

Ietsy was a waitress perched on high heels, purchased specially at the flea market, when his eyes landed on Ninon. She was wearing a long-sleeved sheath dress in white damask inlaid with sparkling jewels, which clung so tightly to her skin that she looked like she was walking around naked, covered in glistening water. She was with a man in a black suit from an equally high-end label, in his forties, his hair as brown as hers was blonde. Ietsy's platter only had a small portion left. Still, he walked over to the couple, slightly out of place among the cross-dressers and the real girls, fresh young things, and thought to himself that he'd gladly part with his molten chocolate cake in exchange for a smile from this siren. Normally, he'd have been too overwhelmed by such beauty to make a move, but the very strangeness of the situation gave him confidence. "There isn't much left, but I can still serve up a nice slice of cake," he said, beaming, and produced a plastic knife to cut the fortuitous piece in thirds. The newcomers smiled too, swallowed the offering in one go, and thanked him.

"Berthe, at your service!" he continued, quickly wolfing down his piece, afraid they'd keep walking.

"Ninon!"

"You're very beautiful," he ventured.

"You too," she replied.

"That's for sure!" agreed her companion, ogling Ietsy from his high heels to the violets on his head, pointedly fixing his gaze on the garter belt.

"Careful," Ninon warned. "Antoine is a real connoisseur!"

"I'm more happy than gay," Ietsy said, smiling to his ancestors.

And that is how they met.

Ninon worked as a model. They'd just gotten out of a function at the Louvre, and she'd wanted to walk down by the water to remind her of the sea where she'd grown up.

There wasn't any champagne left, but Ietsy found a bottle of bordeaux. The glasses were crystal, luckily, from the set Boris's late mother had. They sat on the wall facing the river and talked; the relatively clean concrete didn't seem to repel the nice clothes. Then the friends got out their instruments, started playing songs from *Kind of Blue*, and stopped time. When they began to get tired, or rather thirsty, Antoine took the opportunity to take his leave. Ninon got up too, but her friend assured her that it was okay, smiling amiably at Ietsy, and she stayed.

They talked for a long time about nothing at all, her laughing at his stories and him nodding at what she said, until a cool breeze made her shiver. Ietsy put his bomber jacket around her shoulders. She still wanted to leave, had an early train to catch the next morning. He offered to take her home on his motorcycle, but she said she'd rather walk. So he walked her home. He'd gotten runs in his stockings long before but hadn't considered changing.

She lived on the Rue de Babylon in a top-floor studio. He didn't go upstairs, but they spent a long time in the entryway. Then they squeezed each other's hands. He left, skipping and jumping on his high heels, and did a lap around the public park in front of all the buildings, his hands in the air like a cyclist who'd won the crucial mountain stage but forgotten his bike. Her phone number was in his garter. Looking up to a window at the very top of the building where a light had just turned on, he thought he saw a shadow laugh.

It was just before a long weekend. She'd told him she'd be spending it in the countryside. He hadn't wanted to ask whom with. For the next three days, which stretched out indefinitely, as if trying to make Ietsy understand the theory of relativity, he swung from euphoria, reliving the moment of delicate, stocking-run happiness, to doubt, reliving the same events but picking out contradicting excuses behind every word they'd exchanged, every move Ninon had made. Monday evening, when he called her, he got her answering machine twice in a row. He didn't know what to say to it. Then, gearing himself up to talk to the machine, he called again only to reach Ninon. She was glad to hear from him. He rediscovered the breezy tone he'd had with her on the banks of the Seine. She'd spent the weekend resting and getting ready for a busy week. They set a date to see each other the following Thursday after she got out of a fashion show, this time in a fancy hotel.

He arrived at the appointed hour, a little early even, but since that type of event always runs long, he had to wait at the bar for over an hour. The servers eyed him suspiciously as he ordered drinks like a prince, a black guy with white pretension, but they were overcome with murderous envy when Ninon appeared, breathless but smiling, and headed straight for him.

Ietsy, slightly self-conscious in a brown shirt with small green flowers instead of his usual polo, was instantly buoyed by the kiss she planted easily on his lips. He didn't generally give too much thought to his clothes, but that evening, he thanked his aunt Christiane from the bottom of his heart for bringing him that lovely and not-too-showy shirt from her last trip. He still had his jeans, his leather boots, and the bomber jacket, also from Christiane, which he wore more often, given the way he got around. He'd spent a bit more time than usual getting dressed. He hadn't wanted anyone to take him for one of those *sapeur* dandies he despised so much, even if he sometimes couldn't help but admire the living tableaux they made on the Rue de Strasbourg. He certainly spoiled nothing of Ninon's allure, who this time was wrapped up like a piece of candy in a billowing transparent plastic top. Underneath, she was wearing a mandarin-collared blue crepe de Chine shift with a wide belt casually draped around her waist. A pair of high-heeled thong sandals elevated the arches of her feet sensually, raising Ietsy's blood pressure a notch.

"Sorry for making you wait," she said with a huge smile.

"No problem. You look amazing!"

She wanted to get a drink with some friends, just not in this "tacky" place. Which she pointed out by looking over her shoulder at the customers around them. Ietsy, who'd already done his rounds and hadn't seen anything particularly abhorrent—mostly very chic women and busy businessmen—nodded obligingly. While he settled his bill, Ninon's friends turned up with a brutal gust of fresh air. Following them out, he glanced back around the room one last time and felt like he understood what Ninon had meant.

The other girls hopped into a taxi, and Ninon hopped up behind Ietsy on his motorcycle. He'd brought a helmet for her, but she said she wanted to feel the wind. "Screw the cops." Ietsy took off, cackling.

Parisians in their cars usually didn't spare much attention for bikes, but that night, they seemed the model of common courtesy. She shone like a beacon. They got off the bike on a street near Les Halles, and Ninon took his arm. He was just starting to get used to people turning around to stare as they went by, and then in the café, especially when the other girls breezed in all aflutter, he could clearly see the esteem in the eyes of their waiter.

He thought he should have Ninon come with him those three times per year he had to go to the prefecture to renew his student visa. But he knew that would have been out of line, so he tried to crack jokes, stay lighthearted. When he noticed the other girls were barely listening to him, he just smiled.

The trendy bar, the creation of a famous designer, radiated, reflected, and refracted light. There were mirrors all over the place and polished metal everywhere else. He thought it was just as "tacky" as the fancy hotel, just with a younger clientele. Still, when he went to take a piss, into what seemed like a wall of water, he was absolutely grateful for his luck.

Back upstairs, he found, like clouds hanging over his starry sky, two guys who'd sat down with the girls. He introduced himself with a smile. One of them looked like he knew Ninon very well. He invited all of them to a party he was throwing the next day. They all chattered away. Ietsy tried to follow the conversation and maintain his good mood. On the way home, he forgot all the others very quickly when Ninon, hands clasped around his waist, rested her head on his back.

Once they reached the Left Bank, she asked him to stop and walk a bit. Ietsy parked in front of a police station. The officer on guard outside saw them without helmets and was visibly happy to answer Ninon's dazzling "good evening." After locking up his motorcycle, Ietsy skipped gaily over to her. She took his hand and kept it in hers.

"Do you want to go to Paul's party tomorrow?"

"If you want," he said. "He seems chill."

"That's cool of you. He's my ex."

"Oh!"

There were hardly any people around anymore. He caught hold of her and peered carefully at her, trying to see who was there behind that beauty, the mouth that smiled wide and often under dimples, her impish nose that could question the weather itself, her high cheekbones highlighting her round forehead, and her eyes, between blue and gray, oh ancestors, that drank in everything. Headlights occasionally lit Ninon's face. Yet he seemed to glimpse a shadow behind her eyes. He smiled weakly, and a "Yeah, if you want" tumbled out. She offered him her lips, and he tasted them. First like a forbidden fruit, the hint of a kiss. When she didn't pull them away, he had more. A mouthful. He felt molten steel flow through him, burning and freezing at the same time.

For the rest of the way to her place, they didn't say anything more about the other guy. She asked him what he thought of her friends. They're nice, he said. You mean they're dumb? I don't know. You're not like them. What am I like? Why are you with me? Tread lightly, Ietsy thought.

As soon as they got to the entryway, she warmed up. She kissed him before bounding up the stairs two at a time. "Here," she said, giving him her purse. "Careful with that, my whole life's in there!" He let himself get left behind. But she didn't want to lose him. She turned on one of the landings and came back down to kiss him again.

"Let's make love," she told him.

"I am blessed by the Gods and Ancestors," Ietsy said.

"Get undressed and wait in bed for me." She giggled as she pushed him into her room. She joined him a few minutes later, slipping under the sheets after having turned off all the lights and taken off her robe. She'd laughed her little laugh, so seductive. Did he want to respect the modesty she'd displayed? Was he afraid to discover the hidden marvels? Whatever it was, he said nothing, touching her in the faint glow of the Parisian night sky. He feasted on Ninon's full, supple body, so unlike the matchstick models in vogue. She hardly tried to move, only turned over when he was about to take her. He had a moment's hesitation, which she cut off by thrusting her hips back, rubbing up against him. "This is my thing," she whispered, clutching his head against her neck. His pleasure had barely begun when it had come and gone. Embarrassed, he pulled out. He thought he could beg forgiveness by reverently kissing the shoulder at his mouth, stroking her face. He tried to kiss her lips again, but she turned her head. Then he noticed furtive movement. When she started gently moaning, he literally prayed to her through closed lips on her skin. Fear and awe chilled his blood and all his senses as she stirred her

70

arm faster and faster, even elbowing him sometimes, which he took unflinchingly like presents to connect them. Both of them were breathing hard when she finally pressed herself to him, jamming her foot into his ankle, and unveiled paradise to him for a few dazzling seconds. Satisfied, a smile playing on her lips, she sank into him and fell asleep.

His eyes stayed wide open and his body motionless for the better part of the night, thoughts tumbling around in his head. He put up with the tingling arm he'd threaded under Ninon's neck for a long time without daring to change his position. His mouth dried up just at the sight of this young woman sleeping. He wanted to stay like that until she awoke, but back then, sleep always overtook him eventually.

When he woke up, he didn't feel her next to him and immediately sensed danger. She was drinking her coffee calmly, leaning against a little table in the next room, in sight of the bed. She said good morning as if nothing had happened. From where Ietsy was lying, he could see her bare toes fidgeting, strangely independent from her feet. She was getting ready to leave for a long day of photo shoots. Ietsy, still in disbelief about his night, both sated and tormented, wondered how she could be so radiant so early in the morning.

"How'd you become a model?" he managed to ask without leaving the bed.

"When I finished at Sciences Po," she said, "I worked in the marketing department of a major food company. One day I was working on a new campaign for carbonated water with the publicist, Antoine, you actually know him, and he convinced me that what it needed was a girl like me. I took the plunge. I'd never seen myself modeling. And I won't be doing it forever, either."

She got up to let some air into the apartment, walking by Ietsy, who was still curled up in bed, a low Japanese futon, equally impressed by the young woman's winding career path as by her few simple steps from the table to the picture window. She was wearing a light blue dress that made him think of summer and want to become wind so he could rush beneath it.

"How long have you been doing it?"

"Less than six months. What about you? Why are you in law school?"

"Just because. I didn't really choose it," he admitted.

"And what do you want to do when you grow up?"

"Uh . . . nothing!"

"Nothing?"

Ninon's tone was one of mild ridicule with a hint of curiosity. Ietsy had noticed it, sure, but couldn't think of anything to add. It was what he'd said since he was little, which would make everyone in Anosisoa laugh. His father always laughed last, after his guests, and then would proudly state, "That's my boy!" and laugh again.

"What are you going to live off of?"

"I," he said soberly, "am blessed by the Gods and Ancestors."

"Yeah, you're definitely a daddy's boy, huh?"

Her words utterly crucified him. He didn't know what to say. In the olden days, he'd commanded the respect of his classmates when he explained that doing nothing, for him, was a philosophical project. He wanted to tell Ninon that such a choice would leave him all the time in the world to devote to her. But he could clearly see that independence was an integral part of her personality, and he was more the one who needed her desperately.

Ietsy wasn't in any mood to study for the whole day. Like the previous days but at a faster pace, he swung from euphoria—after all, he was going out with the most beautiful girl in Paris—to dread, because not only did all of Paris want to steal her from him, but she might see his own shortcomings. How could he be at her level when he himself was placing her on a pedestal way above him?

He was supposed to pick her up at her place to go to Paul's party that night, but they hadn't set a time. He forced himself to stay at the library until it closed, then wandered casually over to ring the doorbell in the entryway. She wasn't back yet.

The big-box store next to her place had nothing in the perfume or accessory departments that he found worthy of his sweetheart. There was, however, a fairly well-stocked bookstore inside where he found, all the way on the top shelf, a small, textured ivory treasure from Fata Morgana: *Merina Food and Love*, by Jean Paulhan. How had that book wound up there? Would Ninon like it? In any case, they were about to close.

So, at ten after eight, he was pacing up and down the street again. Waiting exacerbated his doubts. He opened the book to pass the time and was shocked to see what the writer from the Académie Française had thought about long-ago Malagasies.

When she waved wildly at him from her taxi over an hour later, he forgot everything. He even forgot to give her the book, which he put in his bag without a second thought.

She wanted to take a shower, eat something before going out. He smiled at everything she said. He didn't want to be apart from her again, but she laughed and parked him in the living room with a drink.

When she got out of the shower, Ietsy pounced on the robe she was about to slip on. He wanted to see her completely naked, he said, drying her, kissing her, licking the drops of water that still beaded on her face and neck. She laughed her little laughs when he nibbled her. She stood on tiptoe to return his kisses, then grabbed him around his neck. Ietsy finally beheld the desire in her eyes. When he felt one of her delicate feet toying with the hem of his jeans, he pulled them down and took her up against the shower stall. His eyes filled with tears when she screamed her release.

"I want to move soon," she told him later, biting into a piece of cheese. "I like this apartment, I lived in it all through university. It's practical, everything's close by, but it's getting too small."

"Yeah," he said. "Especially the bathroom."

The party was in full swing when they got to Paul's place. He had a nice apartment on the top floor of a cut-stone building on top of Montmartre. Ietsy's nerves had vanished, probably washed away in the shower. Everyone screamed when they saw Ninon. Everyone eyed Ietsy curiously when she introduced him. His eyes still damp, a pleasant and satisfied smile plastered on his face, he was proud to be her chivalrous knight. He even offered Paul a warm handshake, prepared to forgive him for that bit of familiarity, given his past with Ninon. When Ietsy spotted the bar, he left Ninon in full-on conversation with her friends who were dying for news.

She was bantering and flirting all over the place. A dread-locked DJ was plodding away over some old turntables, and a few lonely souls danced a languid reggae beat in front of him. The instant Ninon stepped onto the dance floor, the number of people multiplied. She had a way with her body, just covered in an African wrapper, of moving without moving, both conventional and provocative, surpassing the suggestively shaking hips and other lascivious dance moves around her.

The DJ put on a brilliant, brassy Fela Kuti song, as if to emphasize that Ietsy wasn't the only one keeping an eye on things. Ietsy heard "Trouble Sleep" and, after throwing the guy spinning discs a dirty look, knocked back his glass of Ti-feu and threw himself into the circle around Ninon.

He did his best, but dancing had never been his forte. Back home, it hadn't been a big deal, but here people were merciless. White people thought he should have rhythm in his bones. He'd always liked music, but he didn't play an instrument, and he danced like a broomstick. And yet, with no false shame, he wriggled his way toward Ninon. She laughed when she saw him; he was immensely relieved. The soles of her feet were tapping the ground like a real African, and the woven silk enveloping her rose like a wave to her chest and broke over her bare shoulders, waking the three copper serpents twisting around her left arm. "They don't leave my arm," she'd told him the first night when he'd mentioned how they resembled the guardians of the old royal idols in his country.

"We call them *marolongo*," he'd said. "Those-with-Many-Accomplices. They live several to one hole and are sacred to us. They say that if anyone kills one of them, the others will track the unrighteous man to his home and strangle him in his sleep."

"Really? I bought them in Senegal. The merchant told me always to wear them together. I thought he just wanted to foist all three of them on me at the same time."

And she laughed, luring Ietsy with the liquid sound emanating from her throat as much as with her clinking rattlesnake bracelets that had long ago hypnotized His Majesty's subjects. He found no handhold to grab. Since then he'd been slipping, slowly, with a certain intoxication, under beautiful Ninon's power, like a man letting himself succumb to vertigo.

"You dance like a queen," he whispered in her ear, taking the opportunity to nibble on her lobe.

"You're like the royal scepter!"

She giggled as she kissed him, lingered on his lips, not disapproving of him.

"Tastes good," she said. "What did you have to drink?"

"Rum with lime and brown sugar."

"Mmm! Can you make me one?"

He nodded, pleased to be of some use to her. Heading for the bar, he saw that the DJ had abandoned his post. That was fine; Fela had the floor for a bit, and he never half-assed anything. Ietsy found the ingredients he needed but rejected the plastic cups and made his way to the kitchen to find some real glasses. When he got back, Ninon wasn't on the dance floor. The Nigerian master was still dropping his Afrobeats. Ietsy felt happy and light. He finished mixing the fiery cocktail.

He went out onto the balcony to get some fresh air. There wasn't any light, but his nose immediately picked up the distinctive aroma that had filled his adolescent head, a scent of burnt tea and caramelized honey, but there was something else mixed in. Ietsy smiled to think that here they mixed the sacred weed with tobacco. He also recognized the silhouette of the DJ with his dreadlocks, then saw another magnificent profile illuminated by the predawn sky: Ninon. He started to walk toward them, glass for Ninon in hand, when she leaned toward the long-haired man beside her to offer him not the joint that was making them laugh, but her lips. Stunned, Ietsy's heart stopped. He watched her blow a smoke ring at the DJ, who wasn't content with just the smoke but pulled her in for a real kiss. Ninon let it happen. Ietsy staggered back, his cheeks on fire.

He could have walked onto the balcony a minute earlier or later, he thought. He would have walked up to them, held out the glass to Ninon, joked with the guy, maybe even smoked. He would have asked, to earn one of the gorgeous smiles Ninon wore when she was interested in something, if he went out in public with such red eyes because he kept contact with the ancestors. The DJ probably would have said that it was due to his warrior's tears and that he was forced to fight his way through life, so he smoked to endure the atrocities committed and weathered. Ietsy would have warned him about what his grandfather had said about the Ancestors' weed, namely that only initiates could smoke it to appreciate how it opened the mind without falling into the void. The disciple of andzamal may have responded that the rites of reggae had prepared him for that eventuality, for he'd lived through enough to have long hair, hadn't he. And they would have all laughed together.

Ietsy was leaning against the picture windows when someone came up to him. He threw back the Ti-feu intended for Ninon in a single gulp to erase the offense he thought might be read on his face, then forced a smile for his host.

"You wouldn't want to give us a hand to get these drums upstairs, would you?" Paul asked him.

"Sure thing," said Ietsy, who wanted to do anything as long as it didn't make him think of what had just happened on the balcony.

So he went downstairs with Paul and the percussionist to a car parked across from the building. He pulled out a long, ovoid drum and, without a glance up to the balcony hanging over them, carried it up without stopping until he reached the seventh floor. People were gushing over the drums as they set them up. Fela was indefatigable, still singing as strong as his saxophone. Ninon popped up next to Ietsy, eyes alight.

"Do you play the congas?" she said eagerly.

"I just helped get them here," he said without looking up, feigning interest in how the screw tension worked on the Cuban drums.

"Shit, man, you sprang up those stairs like a jackrabbit!" Paul wheezed. He'd finally made it up with the last one.

Ietsy threw him a look with no animosity, but no smile, either, and went to make more Ti-feus at the bar. This time, he used plastic cups. He downed his and brought one to Ninon, who, perhaps thinking herself at the Shrine, was banging on the congas and jumping around in her bare feet. Paul, his musician friend, and the DJ were gazing adoringly at her. All this beauty for my unhappiness, Ietsy thought to himself. It was more than he could bear. He left the drink on one of the congas—such sacrilege!—and went out onto the deserted balcony.

He looked out over the city unfurling before him, trying to figure out which way was north so he knew which way he should be invoking his Gods and Ancestors.

"Admiring Paris?" said Ninon, who'd joined him without him realizing it.

"Yeah," he lied, still leaning against the railing.

"Are you sulking?"

"Is there a reason for me to be sulking?"

Ninon didn't answer, just slipped into his arms. "If you aren't sulking, you should look at me, not Paris," she told him.

He gave a cowardly smile and closed his eyes so he would neither obey her nor exactly disobey her. "I'm tired," he finally muttered.

"Then let's go!" she said, nestling up to him even more closely.

He held her tightly, full of appreciation. They didn't leave right away. Yet, as day was breaking, he still had the privilege of going home with her.

Nights like that happened once, twice a week all the way up to school break, with variations on the theme. Sometimes he left by himself around one in the morning, sometimes before midnight, and sometimes he didn't go at all.

"I'm jealous," Ietsy said.

When he'd asked her for a little more time for them, she'd reiterated to him, "You're part of my life." He should have been grateful. Wherever Ninon went, she created a cheerful environment around her, kind of like how Mr. Razak imposed subservience around himself. All Ninon had to do was flash her sparkling eyes and the neighbor, cop, street sweeper, anyone would put a smile on their face, blocking out clouds, pollution, and all the other stresses of the big city. Ietsy felt even more devastated when she went away. Sometimes as bowled over as the ticket inspector on the metro who'd had the misfortune of trying to impede Ninon's brilliant path. Looking back on that as he lay on the guest bed in Anosisoa, unable to shut his eyes, he smiled fondly and then burst out laughing.

She hadn't been able to find her yellow ticket at the RATP turnstiles. But she ignored the one Ietsy was holding out to her and shamelessly snuck in behind an indulgent passenger. On the train, without fail, an agent busted her and informed her that there would be a fine. She put on a whole show as if she had a stamped ticket in her purse, and she dumped everything out, old tickets, various notebooks, pens, cigarettes, newspapers, books, makeup, pain meds, bobby pins, pictures, cards, keys, glasses—it all came out before the dazed agent, whom she was also teasing and insulting, and when the train finally arrived at her stop, she pulled out a 200-franc note and threw it in his face, shouting, "There's your payment!" over her shoulder as she flounced out the door under Ietsy's amused, then protective eyes—"You got what you wanted, now leave her alone"—while everyone else in the car looked like they wanted to follow Ninon to her dressing room to congratulate her.

Ietsy dreamed that she would bring him with her in her purse along with all the other objects lost at the bottom the way individual days and nights get lost in a life: that she'd use him to hold back her hair instead of the bobby pins she could never find; that she'd keep him like the old movie and theater tickets, or that popsicle stick, a souvenir of an afternoon with her father, their first outing since her younger brother was born, when she got accepted into Sciences Po and moved to Paris; that she'd write on him in place of her notebooks, the title of a book recommended to her, the price of a trip spotted in a window, telephone numbers followed by names or vice versa, even guys' names, that she'd scribble them all on him; that she'd fidget with him in her hands instead of a pen; that she'd smoke him greedily between photo shoots; that she'd read him fervently in the back of a taxi, yes, him instead of Cioran, whose ideas, he'd warned her, could transform your soul like acid turns the blue tint of litmus paper red—it would be better to watch the cars driving bumper-to-bumper or to chat with the drivers even if none of them could keep themselves from flirting with her; that she'd swallow him in the middle of a fashion show with a sip of water as a migraine tortured her like endless flashbulbs; that she'd set him on the bridge of her nose to protect her eyes from the sun or to use him to see life; that she'd slip him into dead bolts to lock all the doors and stay alone with him.

That was obviously impossible. He wouldn't have been able to handle it, either, despite his fantasies. Because being with Ninon had just as much misery as ecstasy. The life she led, fed, enhanced, it was more of an erupting volcano than a river winding lazily to the sea. Ietsy had to stay alert every moment or else he'd be consumed by molten lava.

She dragged him along to contemporary art exhibits and obscure art-house cinemas, which he found absurd, and had to really focus to appear receptive to them. What exactly was that Japanese film about the woman throwing out the sand that's filling her house, which turns out to be in the middle of a sand world? Or that other one where an actress sips her whiskey endlessly while everyone waits for her for the final scene of the play? Utterly outrageous films. But she demanded to hear his thoughts about them. Same thing leaving the theater, after they'd gone to see a one-woman show about nothing more than spouting forth a bunch of stuff about solitude, like a young girl who just hit puberty watches blood flowing from between her legs, or, a little better in Ietsy's mind, in Nanterre, on a long, narrow stage, two men discussing the price of something that was never revealed, haggling over it for the whole play, masters of dueling with meaningless words. He'd already endured such performances in another life at the simplest of family ceremonies, during which he'd have to stay seated through the whole thing without moving a muscle next to Mr. Razak, who revered that type of thing. Yes, there he could, like Ninon, toss out his final opinion: guys who were just talking to kill other people's time and save their own! And when putting forward that opinion, he had to look her right in the eye, for that was where Ninon's little laugh began, before sliding down to her throat, rising again to pinch her dimples and dying, if she wanted, on Ietsy's lips. He snatched victory out of those nights like in a boxing match. Other times, he lost and left with his heart feeling as if it had been stomped flat.

But whenever Ninon remembered him and set up a date, he always came running. Sometimes his all-consuming fears would be masked with an agreeableness that surprised him. "What do you take me for?" Ninon had retorted one day when he'd suggested using a condom. He didn't answer and dropped the matter. He was probably expecting her to fling her arms around his neck because he'd noticed that every time he feigned any level of detachment, like "You and your friends will have plenty of fun without me," she would be even more infatuated with him. It also helped him not to just mope around and have suspicion gnaw away at him, aimlessly cursing every male and sometimes also every female who was electrified in Ninon's wake.

During this time, he read or played chess with Boris, expounding on the blessed era his grandfather had told him about, before the Christian missionaries arrived, when desire grew like rice seedlings wherever it was planted without offending anyone's heart.

"Back then, they knew that no one belongs to anyone!" he lamented to his friend across the chessboard.

"Yeah! But . . . didn't you tell me your kings had twelve wives?"

"That was for political reasons! Each one on their own hill—there were twelve sacred hills around the capital—each one of them was free to do whatever she wanted. None of our legends are about a man who's sad because he's separated from his beloved," he said bitterly.

"Then why are you beating yourself up?"

"I don't know, probably because I also heard about Tristan and Isolde, and Sleeping Beauty too."

"You think?"

"I mean, it's mostly that . . . she's incredible!"

He breathed.

"And because . . . I love her."

"Have you told her that?"

"Oh, come on, she's already got me on a tight-enough leash!"

In all the games of chess Boris and Ietsy played against each other over all those years, from Bièvres to Versailles, they each won about the same amount. During the Ninon period, however, Ietsy won the tiebreaker every time. As sweet as that was, he had only Ninon on his mind. He also managed to get his master's degree by some miracle.

"You are truly blessed by the Gods and Ancestors," Boris had admitted.

"Maybe I'm just a lucky devil."

Then, in a seemingly unrelated vein, he continued.

"Actually, I do know several Malagasy legends where there's a lover pining for his sweetheart. Paulhan was the one who didn't want them to exist . . . I would have liked that too! Even in the myth of Ibonia, there's a child who decides to leave his mother's womb to go after his betrothed who'd been captured by a rival."

"He sounds like he's taking action, not sitting around beating himself up, right?"

"Yes," Ietsy admitted. "The problem is that all these stories tell you how to get the girl, but none of them says what to do next!"

"Probably live happily ever after and have lots of children," Boris said.

"How? Now all the pretty girls can live happily ever after by themselves."

As he moved his hand toward the chessboard, Ietsy recalled the riddle of Rasarotrafoitoavary, She-Who-Is-as-Difficult-to-Leave-Behind-as-Rice.

"Her name can also be translated as 'a brutally beautiful woman,'" Ietsy said. "She was so tempting that anyone who saw her couldn't take their eyes off her. She asked all her suitors, all those who'd seen her, to bring her the hearts of their parents, both of them, mama and papa. Not a single one balked. They backed away slowly, devouring her with their eyes as they left. Then they rushed back, famished, their hands still dirty. They presented their bloody tributes to her, some with heifers' hearts, calf hearts, some with monkey hearts, their neighbors' hearts, even the two hearts of their parents, both of them, mama and papa. She threw them all out of her house, warning the people that there were assassins prowling the city!" He laughed with his friend, then said, "What do I need to bring Ninon?"

"I have no idea what goes on inside chicks' heads," Boris confessed, once again tipping over his king.

At the beginning of July, after leaving her at a party, Ietsy decided not to go back to Versailles and went to wait for her in her building's entryway, his heart wasting away. "You're insane," she told him when she found him freezing at dawn. He didn't regret it. That morning, she loved him like never before. When he woke up—she always woke up earlier than he did—she brought him brunch in bed, a tray with croissants, melon, toast, bacon, and scrambled eggs, and said they should spend a weekend out by her parents in Saint-Malo.

"You can't stay at the house because it'll be a little tricky with my father," she said. "We'll get a hotel room nearby."

"Works for me," he said, putting sugar in his coffee.

Then, before he drank it, he started to worry.

"What do you mean that it'll be tricky with your father?"

Ninon laughed, making the tray rattle on his knees. "He's particular about my boyfriends. I'm his only daughter. You get it?"

"Not really. But I'm happy to come if you want me to, and . . . I'll find out."

Ninon's father owned one of the most prosperous oyster-farming companies in the area, and according to Ninon, he enjoyed recalling how he'd earned his beds through hard work and waking up early every morning. His wife handled the finances and administrative work at first, before they were able to hire more employees beyond the indispensable laborers.

"I helped out too, until the year I took the Bac," Ninon explained. "My little brother, Maxime, is the only one who got out of it. He arrived during the years of plenty. He's spoiled rotten."

Ietsy smiled, tried to picture Ninon on a tractor in huge boots and a yellow slicker, and laughed out loud.

"Why are you laughing?" Ninon huffed.

"I can't see you on an oyster farm. When I visited Mont-Saint-Michel with my father, I saw a bunch of farmers on the tidal flats working their beds—it's a hard job!"

"So? What do you think of this?"

She flexed her delicate arms.

"Mostly," she added, "I did sales at supermarket entrances with one of my cousins around Christmastime and over school vacations. That was a hard job too!"

So, they went to Saint-Malo the day before the July 14 holiday. Ietsy had traded his bike for Boris's car, and they headed up the vacation highway like everyone else. The weather was gorgeous, unlike the stormy mood inside the car.

For one thing, the traffic jams leaving the city tried everyone's patience, but the trip was mostly polluted with animosity mixed with some anxiety. When Ietsy had gotten to Ninon's the night before, he'd had the unpleasant surprise of meeting her cousin there. Marc. He was studying business in Paris and wanted to hitch a ride to go see the family.

"I hope that doesn't bother you," Ninon had said.

"Oh no, not at all," Ietsy grumbled.

In his own easygoing way, this cousin presented an undeniable problem for Ietsy: he and Ninon had a shared history dating back to the oyster farm years, and he was constantly trying to bring her back there, like he was trying to exclude Ietsy.

As if that wasn't enough, Ninon no longer seemed too sure that she really wanted to introduce Ietsy to her family, or conversely, her family to Ietsy. The farther they got from Paris, the more she entrenched herself in Saint-Malo talk with her cousin, as if she was wary of the intruder at the wheel. Her tone of voice when addressing Ietsy, even to say perfectly ordinary things, showed marked devaluation. He wasn't used to being treated in such a manner and was seething with rage as he drove but strove to put on a happy face. Marc, perhaps finally figuring out the situation, stopped talking and took a nap. Ninon pretended she was getting drowsy to avoid talking to Ietsy, and eventually fell asleep.

As they neared Saint-Malo, Ietsy woke up his passengers to ask where they were dropping off the cousin.

"He'll be going to my parents' for drinks too," Ninon said. "We'll drop off our bags at the hotel first, and then we can all go there together."

"Okay. Am I heading downtown?"

"Yes, I got a room by the port."

The Old Beachside Hotel featured turn-of-the-century gables, solid and opulent. When they checked in, the man at reception assured them that it had been rebuilt as an exact replica after the war. The bed took up almost the entire room, and there was a nice view overlooking the walled city and an antique claw-foot bathtub in the adjoining room, to Ninon's great delight.

"I'm going to take a bath," she said, sweeping into the bathroom and locking the door.

Ietsy stretched out on the bed. He would have loved to join her, but it still felt like she was trying to keep some distance between them. And on top of it all, Marc was still getting underfoot: now he lay down next to Ietsy, completely unbothered. The receptionist had eyed them suspiciously, piquing Ietsy even more. He closed his eyes.

When they went to get the car, Ietsy was tired of driving and asked if they couldn't just walk there.

"There aren't any oyster farms here!" Ninon said with a laugh. "Follow the signs to Cancale."

Her laughter, even at his expense, made Ietsy relax a little, so he just agreed and started driving, not about to give her cousin the wheel.

It took under half an hour to reach the family's villa. The house looked like the ones Ietsy had seen on American TV shows that smelled like new money. A long cobblestoned drive wound around to the back of the house. Two cars were already parked outside, one a huge SUV, in front of a massive speedboat on a trailer. Ietsy pulled in behind them. There were a few people sitting at a table and some kids playing on the patio, watching them get out of the car. A short brunette boy, maybe ten years old, raced into the house, shouting, "Ninon! Ninon's here!"

Instantly, Ietsy felt shut out of the family circle. It had nothing to do with the feeling he got at the prefecture where he was magnanimously handed his one-year residency extension with a start date of five or six months earlier. There, the papers and glass counter windows, both a means of communication and a screen between Ietsy and the civil servant, kept their relationship to a forgiving abstraction. The administrative decision was "nothing personal," as he often heard explained to people less fortunate than he, even when it determined not only the beggar's residency status but usually their entire life too. There, the bureaucratic motives were too far removed from those involved to envision, much less tolerate, a response with any degree of humanity. The clerk would slide their little glass window shut or simply leave their desk, or, if an immigrant raised their voice about the prefectural order resembling a guillotine, would call security.

No one on the patio was paying any attention to Ietsy. Ninon rushed to hug her parents, then aunt, uncle, brother, and friends of the family. They all gave her and Marc a long, warm welcome, as if to delay the moment of greeting the stranger. It'll be better in a minute, Ietsy thought, wagering that Ninon would eventually introduce him. His bubble of hope quickly burst: Ninon's little brother dragged her inside to show off his new video game console. Ietsy felt abandoned, a clam left in the sun at low tide. But then Marc scooped him up like nothing had happened, gesturing to him without giving any details besides his name.

They saw fit at that point to glance at him, but everyone looked like they were waiting to see Ninon's father's reaction before saying anything. The patriarch, as tall as Ietsy but built much more imposingly, with a large, round face that could harden in an instant, stepped forward and, after casually brushing his straight brown hair off his forehead, held out his hand.

"Ah!" he said, a smile emerging on his face as if he was getting ready to tell a grand joke. "You're also a business student, then?"

"Um, I'm a law student," Ietsy said, afraid to try anything more to remedy the contempt that everyone wanted to ignore.

Everyone seemed to tacitly admit him as Marc's friend, welcoming him as such. Marc's stepfather, Ninon's father's sister's partner if Ietsy had understood it correctly, came over to tell him that he'd studied law too. At Bordeaux. He started discussing the so-called merits of the Parisian university that was administering Ietsy's education.

"Well, Assas is the most righteous, rightful law school in France, and rightly so!" Ietsy managed to interject—he couldn't care less about that argument.

He left the man speechless and turned to see if Ninon was back outside. He accepted a drink from a woman, maybe Ninon's mother or stepmother, a little more cordial than the patriarch but not going out of her way to elucidate Ietsy's ambiguous status. As usual, Ietsy settled with giving her a small smile. He turned back to the legal expert to see if he'd finally managed to swallow his peanut.

"Very good!" he exclaimed, raising his glass toward Ietsy. "Ha ha ha! Very good!"

"What are you laughing about?" Ninon called as she came outside.

Ietsy took her arm and lowered his voice as he led her away. "I was telling this gentleman that Marc has a nice ass, which made it worth coming all the way out here."

"What kind of nonsense is that?"

"Nothing," he said, winking back at the uncle, who was still laughing as he watched them walk away.

The bewilderment on Ninon's face gave him a few moments of delicious, ridiculous revenge. Beneath his artificial cheer, he was incensed that he couldn't tell her everything that had been bugging him since they'd left Paris. Plus, he blamed her for being aware of it without raising a finger to do anything about it. At dinner he was put next to the little brother and across from Marc, unable to get into the circle closing around Ninon and her father.

He exploded in the car when, just as they were about to leave to see the Nocturnes light show at Mont-Saint-Michel, as they'd been planning since this trip took shape, Ninon pushed it further.

"Wait," she said as he started the car, "Marc's on his way."

"On his way? He's coming with us?"

"Of course!"

Ietsy felt completely trapped. Seeing her cousin coming, he locked all the doors out of sheer reflex.

"What are you doing?" Ninon asked him testily.

"I want to be alone with you."

"Open the doors!" she snapped with rising hostility.

Ietsy looked at her and saw dark, rigid will beneath her light, almost transparent skin. Did he have to take everything she did?

"Unlock this car," she squealed, irritation making her voice verge on shrill.

An eternity passed while they sized each other up, and Marc, unable to open the door, rapped on the window. Annoyed by the noise, Ietsy unlocked the doors.

"I wasn't expecting this," he said softly.

"What were you expecting?" Ninon spat, her tone so harsh and forced that it scared him.

"I'm going to the hotel to get my bag. I'll go home tonight. You can come get your things too, if you want. I'll bring you back here before I go." The words gushed out of him without any regard for Marc, who had just slid into the back seat.

His declaration was met with stupor that he took as assent, so he took off. He endeavored to concentrate on his driving and what he'd said, but a thousand thoughts were swirling in his head and a thousand and one emotions were tearing his heart apart. Plus, with the crowds that had come out to see the fireworks, traffic became heavier the closer they got to the city center. Jaw clenched, eyes riveted, he fought to calm his jittery driving and pushed forward by instinct, lurching between prudence and speeding.

He double-parked in front of the hotel and left them frozen in their seats. They hadn't said a word and still seemed in disbelief over what was happening. He quickly came down with the bags, put his in the trunk and Ninon's beside Marc in the back. The trip back to Ninon's parents' passed in the same heavy silence, unlike the festive atmosphere on the streets.

"Sorry," Ietsy mumbled as he leaned over to open Ninon's door.

She remained mute as she got out, followed by Marc with her bag.

Ietsy took off again, his tires squealing out of the driveway, picked the least crowded streets, and on the edge of the city when he could accelerate, put the pedal to the floor, and let out a rhinoceros wail. He blew a red light by accident, then the next two on purpose. Motorcycle cops followed after him. He went even faster, running three more lights with them, and didn't stop until he was far away from that damn villa. He turned off the car and got out with his hands in the air; the police hadn't even gotten a chance to unholster their weapons.

Then the tears came. Without trying to hide or dry them, he complied with everything the police said, got hit anyway, which let him scream his pain beneath the colorful, jubilant thunder in the sky. He got sent to a cell, was hit again, went before the judge, did three months of community service at the Garches hospital, was all the same spared extradition—a random impulse would never extinguish his luck.

Stagnating, apathetic, he forgot to register for the next semester, so he couldn't provide all the necessary documents for a new residency card. He became an illegal immigrant through sheer indifference. He lived like that for a little over a year; it was all relative at the beginning because he had the same address and bank account. He made false reports to his family when they asked. He gave up the bike to avoid the all-too-frequent checkpoints. He didn't go too far from the apartment in Versailles. Where would he have gone?

"One time, in a concrete jungle, I followed the sun," he liked to say, like an old zebu whose hide had been tanned by life.

Outside of the walks or bike rides that Boris forced him to take through the woods, he didn't leave the house at all. He stayed in his room, his walls covered in a pretty salmon-pink wallpaper by his friends when he'd been carrying out his sentence from the Garches court, to take his mind off things. He languished through *In Search of Lost Time*, all seven volumes, without getting out of bed except to steal out in the middle of the night when he was sure he wouldn't come across anyone on the way to the bathroom or to get leftovers in the kitchen. His friends, tired of his ever-increasing depression, didn't even notice his bad habits anymore.

He wanted to get out of it, they thought, but he didn't know how. Caroline, Boris's new girlfriend, told him he just had to get out there; Boris, though, recommended the *Journey*. Sometimes, he allowed himself to voice his thoughts that there was really only one way out.

"But I'm not sure I'll take it," Ietsy said.

"You're being an idiot," Boris said. "One tear shed per page is enough."

Other books kept him company during those sleepless hours, bleak writers like Pessoa, whom he learned to appreciate, and Rabearivelo, whom he rediscovered.

In the first, he believed he found the key to weightlessness, painful sores forming on his skin from lying down for so long.

In the second, he looked for the path to an old village. Rabearivelo came from Ambatofotsy Avaradrano, like his mother. When he opened the little book of poetry, his mind was transported down the sunlit path to the right of the Sabotsy Namehana market that led to the deserted yellow lands of the hazy Sundays of his youth.

They'd gone to the old brick church the third Sunday of every month and the Sunday of *vokatra* at the beginning of the harvest period, when the collection is mostly made up of the meager offerings the worshippers lay at the altar in a long procession, while from high in his chair, the pastor counts how many scattered children still remember the Land of the Ancestors. Ietsy recalled how, after the morning at the church, his father would go with him behind the long wall resurfaced in white, leaving the orderly garden behind for one of brambles and wild rosebushes. Agave plants lined the path that led to a door hidden in a wall of red earth, which surrounded the empty space around the vault of his mother's familial line. Sometimes, their excursion pushed deeper into the rustic desolation, all the way to Rabearivelo's tomb. He remembered that they weren't supposed to talk about it, because even with the pride of having such an illustrious neighbor, thus an ally, a relative, it was not morally appropriate to admire such a great poet, for he had, when it came down to it, deliberately chosen death over polite ennui. Ietsy tried to draw words out of the poems in *Translated from the Night* that could elucidate his descent into darkness, hoped to find markers from the past to figure out where he was now.

When Boris realized that Ietsy was intentionally plummeting to rock bottom within himself in the inexpressible hope that then he wouldn't be able to go anywhere but up, he let him go, only giving him an encyclopedia of cooking because, as he'd written on the title page after leafing through his friend's book of hainteny, he had to "be like the zebu, graze and bellow at the same time, for melancholy does not fill the stomach."

One day, Caroline successfully sent Ietsy out to buy groceries. She was hoping to make him graze, like the zebu, with a craving for spicy grilled shrimp and avocado puree, which he'd normally want to have with corn chips, and he and his wild thoughts went to bellow under the white light of their residential shopping center. Leaving the supermarket, Ietsy ran into an ID checkpoint. He dropped his bags and fled with a pack of police officers on his heels. Fortunately, he knew the layout of the neighborhood better than they did; he dashed into the huge parking garage, losing them in the underground maze of corridors with heavy fire doors, made it to their building, raced up the concrete staircase, then the marble one, threw open the apartment door, rarely locked, and slammed it shut, out of breath and shocked he hadn't been caught. He shut himself up in his room without a word.

"I'm telling you," Boris told him through his door, "the police weren't running a checkpoint. It was because of your hairy face, it scared a woman in the frozen aisle, she called them."

"I just wanted spicy grilled shrimp!"

The winter had lasted too long. He made a lifesaving decision the next morning to reascend his Andriba. After a visit to the barber, he enrolled in a new master's program since he couldn't fix the missing year in his file for a doctorate. Then he picked up the phone and called his uncle Jean, who could pull some strings.

It was almost the end of the summer already. On the way out of the prefecture, he ran into Antoine, who was easily persuaded to give him Ninon's phone number. It was the same one Ietsy had. She hadn't changed it.

Ietsy's phone call surprised her, but she listened. The possibility that Ninon could have suffered somehow after his impromptu departure from Saint-Malo hadn't crossed Ietsy's mind. When he apologized, he was thinking more of his, in hindsight, nonchalant attitude. They talked for a long time, even broached the idea of theoretically seeing each other again, but hung up without setting a date. A week later, he called her again. It sounded like she had people over for dinner. Yet she seemed happy to chat with him. He almost managed to extract a date from her, or at least the place she'd be the following night.

Bands just starting out played Clé des Champs to work up their act before facing a larger audience. It was in the nearby suburb of Yvelines. Boris and Caroline had planned on going there and opportunely suggested that Ietsy go with them.

"Why not?" Ietsy replied casually, firmly believing in re-enchantment.

The bands, good ones, cycled on and off stage, and he repeated the first words he'd say to her. He accepted the drink that Boris offered him, but only after some thought. He didn't want to drink too much before being with her because he didn't want to get muddled during the repartee that would most certainly occur. But on the other hand, a small beer would help him relax. Ninon's perpetual petulance required both a clear head, to give as good as she gave, and a joking tone, and indifference, to chase the looming specter of ennui away from her.

On the phone the day before, he'd been extraordinarily successful in captivating her attention, splashing in some humor, making her forget her guests even with the echoes of boisterous conversations and bursts of laughter reaching his ear. The magic enclosing them in their own bubble had been dangling by a thread from the receiver, and he'd have to reattach it this evening, in the middle of this supercharged crowd where the hunters were indistinguishable from their prey, where the boys' eyes reflected in all the girls' eyes, where he had to look like he was having fun even though he was actually horribly nervous.

"It's good to see you again," she said when she saw him. "Don't you remember you're part of my life?"

It had gone much more smoothly than he'd imagined. As if Ninon had only been waiting for a sign from him.

Later, during his insomniac nights in Anosisoa, Ietsy no longer remembered if it was in that period that Ninon revealed to him what she expected from a romantic relationship. According to her, love that was based on trust should not be confined within a couple, but should instead allow each individual to blossom and give the other person strength to explore the world and life.

"Everyday life kills love," she insisted. "It's better if each person has their own life and they see each other every so often, in order to truly appreciate when they're together."

"So, a partner is a drum hanging on a hook by the door, which the master of the house takes down when he wants to express his joy," Ietsy translated.

"Oh, you don't get it at all!" Ninon laughed. "It's more like a grade school crush. In class, we do our work, we look at each other from across the room, we pass notes. Then, at recess, we chase each other, we play jacks to let our hands touch, and we share a snack."

Ietsy wanted to fill his life with his desire for Ninon. For her, obviously, one life, one single life, no matter how vast, could never hold her hunger for the world. Ietsy didn't realize until many years later that she had opened him up to the world.

But for the moment, Ninon was his angel of destruction. Sure as summer gave way to autumn, when flames were unleashed upon the trees.

Late September. Ietsy persuaded her to go to the English Channel for a weekend of sailing with his friends. Ninon wasn't about to give up partying the night before. They agreed she would meet them in Versailles the next day to avoid the traffic. Around noon, the group was all set, the car packed, and no Ninon. Ietsy called her, actually woke her up. She was annoyed, told him she wanted to rest, and hung up with no other explanation. Ietsy called back and heard a man's voice bark, "Hello? Hello?" That time, Ietsy was the one who hung up, distraught. He felt like he was being kept alive artificially, far from his land and his ancestors.

"Go without me," he told his friends. "I have to see her."

"We'll wait for you," Boris reassured him. "Take the car."

The streets were fairly empty going into the city. He drove toward Paris to the Pont de Sèvres, took the Right Bank to Concorde, crossed the plaza and the bridge toward the Assemblée Nationale. It took less than an hour to get to Ninon's street. He rang the buzzer, but no one opened the door. He buzzed again and left his finger on the button. A woman who was going out to walk her dog came out, and he shoved past her into the opening, leaving the scandalized woman behind him, and ran up the stairs two at a time. He rang the bell, pounded the door, but again, no one opened it. He pressed his ear to the door to listen inside. Once he was convinced there was no one there, he went back downstairs and waited outside.

It was hot. He kicked the parking meter instead of putting coins in. There weren't any cafés in her neighborhood, just an empty public park. He was picking up rocks to throw at pigeons when they turned up on the street corner. They were carrying takeout from the nearby Thai restaurant. Ietsy had been there with Ninon before and recognized the white plastic bags with red dragons on them. Ninon seemed very happy, and the guy, with dreadlocks, maybe the DJ from that night a while back, held her arm firmly. Ietsy dropped the rocks and got closer. They stopped in front of the outer door.

Down in the depths of insomnia, Ietsy had a clear memory of Ninon's acidic look. The content of their conversation, though, had faded in a numbing fog. The precise turning point had slipped from his mind. But he knew that both during that incident and before, ever since the moment her phone number had fallen into his hands in Versailles, he'd been existing in an altered state. He could hear, see, feel, but it was like there was someone else talking, moving in his place.

She walked through the door with the other guy right behind her. Ietsy dashed over too, throwing all his weight to block the door, almost falling flat on his face.

"You should go," she said. "Leave us alone."

"I . . . I thought . . . ," he stammered, not able to finish his sentence.

"You thought what?"

"Nothing," he said, turning to go.

"Those boat shoes make you look ridiculous," she taunted before the door shut behind him with a dull click.

He walked to the car, opened the door, and slumped into the seat. After a time, he didn't know how long, he started the car. He took the Left Bank, missed the exit to go west, and unknowingly ended up on the Périphérique. He hadn't been speeding, but he hadn't been paying attention, either, and didn't notice the traffic had completely stopped.

When he came to, he ordered Boris, "Don't say anything to her!"

Sometime after his defeat, when he left the hospital, the band of spoiled Versailles hepcats threw Ietsy a party. They played Miles—it was just after the master's passing—very loudly until very late at night to the immense displeasure of their neighbors. Boris read a passage from Monfreid, then one from *Trout Fishing in America*, to help him feel the expansiveness of life again. Ietsy smiled weakly—he was still recovering—and, as a thank-you for their warm welcome home, gathered the little strength he had and picked up the *Journey* to read. With a soft bass slap to accompany him, he gave them the passage with Lola in a monotone voice, like a Bible reading, exchanging the word "war" for "love." "I no longer want to die," he concluded, closing the book.

IN THE LIGHT OF RANOUR

At the Andriba's peak, when the din of weapons and the melanite smoke had cleared, the surrounding world revealed itself
to Ietsy Razak. As he slowly became aware that other wills
existed besides his own strung along behind a host of ancestors,
his initial reflex was to put walls up around himself. He sang
like a drunken piano, often shutting himself away in a bubble
outside of time, like the Tom Waits album he left permanently
in his CD player that gave his prison a tinge of melancholy. He
had not loved enough. Not enough.

He later faced the outside world in order to establish dominance over it; the aftereffects of his ascent confused his mind
and prevented him from picturing his relationship as anything
other than a battle of wills, which in that way surely resembled
war, demanding the same courage and self-sacrifice.

He still needed several years not to understand and know,
but to accept and trust. Yes, years, despite not a fake life but

one lived like a dream, unhappy without believing it and happy without knowing it. There were of course vague phenomena that might have opened his eyes. Inexplicable gestures, inopportune tears, absences. But those symptoms, of a life unmastered, of a push toward the light, could only be understood after the fact, even if he was surprised by them. For the journey to redemption is long, and the night is darkest just before the dawn.

He sometimes received letters from Versailles. When he got excited about the enclosed books, the latest releases from around the world, he wrote back. Boris and Caroline had come to visit once. They'd been taking their first vacation since the birth of their first child two years earlier, whom they left in the capable hands of Caroline's parents for a few weeks. That made for a number of firsts to celebrate, and champagne flowed like water.

Near the end of dinner, Ietsy disappeared, leaving his wife with the visitors she barely knew. He'd gotten up from the table, saying he needed to get some fresh air. Boris tried to join him but couldn't find him and came in quickly, because it was a large wild property and he didn't want to cross paths with the grandfather, who'd made quite a severe impression on him.

So, they filled the dinner conversation with every bit of pleasantry as it stretched on toward eternity. Then the Razak children were put to bed, and they went into the sitting room for coffee. As always happened in moments like those, they talked about their children. Boris was trying to ease some of the bitter taste Lea-Nour had from being involuntarily excluded from the shared memories up to that point.

They weren't overly worried.

Boris told stories of their walks along the Seine or through a slumbering Versailles, after drinking exorbitant amounts of his father's best bottles, following the main roads or the tiny lanes intersecting them, shunning their beds where dizziness would accost them the instant they lay down.

Pragmatic Lea-Nour, knowing her guests were tired after spending twelve hours on a plane, suggested they may as well head to their room. To avoid making them feel uncomfortable, she didn't let on that Ietsy was unaccustomed to such overindulgences of alcohol since his return to the Land of the Ancestors.

He didn't come back until the next day, late in the morning, and didn't know what to say, other than that he'd gone out the gate leading back to the rice fields, walked along the Andriamasinavalona dikes until he was welcomed by a ditch for the end of the night. A field-worker who recognized him woke him up so as to avoid the burning sun, then had him drink some coffee and brought him back to Anosisoa.

Everyone laughed. The field-worker was offered some sustenance. Lea-Nour got away with nothing more than a sleepless night. Ietsy was ashamed. To redeem himself, he insisted that Lea-Nour join them on the trip they'd planned to the south.

She let herself be persuaded to abandon her precious studies. Her parents agreed to watch the children, and so all four of them left.

There was no more talk of Versailles. Even Boris gave it up after testing the waters, faced with his friend's clear reluctance. Lea-Nour had a lovely trip with a cheerful, most thoughtful husband, and keen friends who, after all, hadn't come to drink, no matter how much it had been a part of the past they shared with Ietsy. She even could have thought of it as a honeymoon trip, like their guests. Ietsy smiled distantly as he watched his friends' plane take off. It was a temporary remission.

On a stormy night when he let Arthur drag him to a school reunion, he had a mysterious crisis.

After eight years of neither seeing nor writing to each other, the two friends reunited as if they'd never been separated. During his studies abroad, Ietsy had come back to the Land of the Ancestors only once. His father had wanted him to visit other countries. He had come home for the summer after his first year of college, but he'd had to hastily cut his trip short. Arthur had been living in England at the time, and Ietsy had lived the high life with good ol' Nestor in the City of a Thousand Circumstances.

Nestor had been waiting for him at the airport with Mr. Razak. Like everyone else, he was unaware of the young man's involvement in the tragic affair with the pills, so Nestor had remained in good standing with Ietsy's father, who had more or less taken him into his service and couldn't conceal how partial he was toward Thor's muscled methods of fixing certain problems. He was depending on him to help Ietsy get interested in the business, and if necessary, to reinstill the comportment that befitted their lofty position on the ladder in the City of a Thousand Rungs. He feared that his son's universally casual way of speaking in the West had affected his values, not only lacking subtlety but also having only the shaky support of a distant, flat formality. Ietsy had not forgotten what he'd only partially understood during his rosy childhood.

That winter—summer break took place during the Southern Hemisphere's winter—he relished the fact that, after four years out of the country, he was sitting on a higher echelon. He'd taken command of the wheel, like he always did, ousting the driver from his seat.

The driver, for a moment, hadn't known quite how to react with Mr. Razak present. He'd regularly surrendered his seat to Ietsy ever since the boy could reach the pedals without sliding down below the wheel. As a child, Ietsy had always boasted that his father himself let him drive, conveniently leaving out the fact that he never drove downtown or in fourth gear. Now Ietsy was old enough to drive legally, and wasn't his father there in the car with them, and smiling? The driver felt relieved of responsibility and began recounting Ietsy's exploits in the streets of the capital.

As everyone was laughing, he'd added that Ietsy wasn't afraid of anything. "Not even *tody*, which everyone dreads!"

"You're not scared of tody?" Nestor had asked, intrigued.

"What's a tody?"

"Come on, it's the punishment you get if you don't respect life!"

"That's not a real thing!"

"Sure, that's what they say: 'Tody isn't real, it's what we do that comes back around!'"

"Maybe, but I mean it doesn't affect *us*."

Ietsy had chosen his words particularly, to mean himself and his family while excluding the other people he was talking to, the driver and Nestor, who was even more dumbstruck by such audacity.

"It doesn't affect you?"

"Yeah, we're blessed by the Gods and Ancestors!"

Ietsy had looked at his father in the rearview mirror as he said it. Mr. Razak's mustache hairs lit up in a huge smile. He even laughed out loud. And they all laughed. His father still advised that he remember to get some ID pictures so that he could get a driver's license made up for him.

Before he'd even received the official authorization, Ietsy had had a serious accident and caused a pedestrian's death during a *pointe*, a race with a huge purse through the mostly deserted streets of the city in the early hours of the morning after they left the clubs. The firefighters had to use iron shears to cut Ietsy out from behind the steering wheel. He was unharmed. As Nestor retrieved the wad of banknotes, the purse, from where he'd taped them himself onto the roof of the car while the motors revved menacingly just before the furious squeal of tires at the start, he no longer had any problem believing that the Gods and Ancestors were truly protecting Ietsy. Mr. Razak undoubtedly thought the same thing. He still sent his son beyond the seas the very next day to avoid any potential problems.

As for Arthur, after a short-lived stay in England—his parents had sent him there after taking the Bac, but he couldn't adapt to either his bigoted grandparents or the freezing rain—he'd taken a shot at the Tana nightlife and done extremely well. He'd found a burgeoning niche in a cabaret that specialized in discovering new talent—although there was never any problem persuading the biggest names to perform at Noctambule, either.

After the boring, conventional dinner of Sintème alumni, Ietsy, Arthur, and Nestor—who was forging his own path through the world of precious stones—braved the driving rain to go to Noctambule. Vava Mahery was playing, a group of young singers and percussionists who were part of the vazimba revival begun by Olombelo Ricky, searching for the original sound. Arthur said they were very promising.

Ietsy only half listened to them, more preoccupied by the story of Nestor's adventures in the sapphire regions in the south. He was trying to convince Ietsy to invest in Sapphire City.

They were discussing that when Arthur interrupted to say that the group was going to sing a ballad for Ietsy. Gentle light filtered through the cabaret. Only one woman was left onstage. Sitting on a stool, she played a calabash that sounded like soft rain. She smacked it with her palms, tapped her fingers on it, stroked her hair over it. A projector was trained on her hands, which danced over the instrument like girls at a festival, made her long black hair shine as it pitched and rolled like the sea under a full moon and covered her as she set the drum at her feet. Then she rose into the beam of light, expanded it as she opened her mouth. She murmured the legend of the pool of tears. Her smooth voice filled every corner of the room, and ears that had been distracted before now seemed to give in to the sweet, wistful invocation. When she finished, the audience was joined in silence, muffled by the violence of the rain outside, before they burst into enthusiastic applause.

Later, Arthur brought the singer to their table to introduce her to his friends. The young woman knew Ietsy's family but was still surprised by his name, and bluntly asked him if, with such a name, he would undertake the task of breathing new life into the country that had lost it, or if he was content to just profit off the life energy sent his way on each and every person's sneezes. Accustomed as Ietsy was to people taking him to task about his family fortune and history, especially in places where class differences were veiled in alcohol and the cover of night, blurring the distances that were so pronounced during the day, he sidestepped the question by suggesting that the legend belonged to everyone and so anyone could freely claim ownership of it.

"Like Vava Mahery does so well!" he added.

"Don't you think that if your ancestors had continued their search for the mythical wellspring instead of stopping at the mountain of gold and silver, life in this destitute yet rich country would have been better?"

She was getting worked up and raising her voice. Arthur, who thought it ridiculous to judge Ietsy for the choices his ancestors had made, tried to put her words into perspective, but she persisted.

"Have you ever walked on the shores of Lake Itasy? Have you never felt love, that you're so indifferent to everything around you?"

Despite the singer's vehemence, Ietsy could barely hear her questions in the noise of the room. Some of her words, though, like "Itasy" and "indifferent," got through and cut deep into his protective shell. Flustered, not so much by what she was saying but by what he was starting to feel, Ietsy stood up.

Mistaking his intentions, the singer also stood to keep him from getting away. She wanted to stare into his eyes, perhaps to show that she, too, deserved to speak frankly about what she felt, but he turned away. She was examining his life for a trace of the legend whose name he bore but could not see the two dark pools brimming over on his face.

Ietsy knocked over a couple of chairs, and other patrons sprang back from the table as if driven away by a ghost. The door seemed too far away from him, from the fountains spouting from his eyes that he couldn't control and didn't understand. He dropped his head, bored toward the stairs to the bathroom, and dove behind the first open door he found. It took more than fifteen minutes for him to get his emotions in order. The whole time, he wondered what was happening to him and why. Ridiculous thoughts ran through his head as he realized the spring was far from drying up. He reasoned that, having had only one beer, he shouldn't be able to squeeze out three times that volume in tears. Since they continued to flow like an open faucet, he imagined all the drinks he'd ever had and all the water falling from the sky that night. As he finally concluded that there couldn't be a direct link between them, he left the bathroom stall and bowed his head above the sink so he could drown his sobs directly in the water. After a long time, during which six, maybe seven people, united by extraordinary discretion or perhaps a shared base level of hygiene, slipped out without washing their hands, he went back upstairs. Since he hadn't exactly dried up, he hung back in the staircase with the posters of groups who'd appeared at Noctambule. Then he went out into the never-ending rain and, once he was thoroughly wet, jumped into a taxi.

When a worried Arthur called him the next day, he said through his stuffy nose that it was nothing and that everything would be fine. His friend pressed him, but he clammed up. Before hanging up, Arthur asked him if it was the singer who'd bothered him. Ietsy assured him that she'd had nothing to do with it.

His wife easily could have gotten suspicious, but she knew Ietsy. Their bonds were forged even before their births. She accepted these odd moments as consequences of his reportedly turbulent childhood. However, even before they got married, Ietsy did something to her that few women would have stood for: he forgot her.

Coming back from beyond the seas, still on the plane, even before giving him an update on the business, Mr. Razak mentioned Lea-Nour over the course of their conversation, a magistrate friend's daughter, his own goddaughter, whom young Ietsy had played with but, on the brink of adolescence, he'd left behind for other games. Ietsy hadn't wanted to get attached to anything, so he smiled vaguely upon mention of her. But he didn't want to hear his father talk about work, either, nor the preparations to be made for succession. His return was like a rebirth, an eager rediscovery of his privileges—what he called his freedom. His father approved of him having his fun. Ietsy was seen gunning his motorcycle everywhere, his head bare, his eyes protected only by aerodynamic sunglasses. There was usually a girl hanging on behind him. He was at all the best parties and exuded pure fun. Treading the earth of his ancestors, breathing that air, looking at that sky, and above all, seeing the recognition in his compatriots' eyes or attitudes, it was enough for him; the weight of the dead made his life lighter. He took plenty of time before finally approaching the girl who'd shared his childhood games, at a social event in the city.

It had been three years since he returned to the Land of the Ancestors and started cruising through his City of a Thousand Lovers. Lea-Nour was finishing her literature degree. She and her classmates were staging a play called *The Spirits*, where the authors who'd written the history of Malagasy literature visited a young writer who lamented having to build everything from scratch. After premiering at the University of Antananarivo, the play moved to the Civic Theater, recently renovated by the French foreign aid service. It had a huge impact for a society that had lost its bearings and encouraged people to rediscover older authors. During a post-performance discussion, Lea-Nour emphasized that, on the contrary, *The Spirits* meant to clear a space for new voices among the shadows of the past and lights from the outside.

At the renovated theater, the audience included some members of the French foreign aid service who'd come to open it with the mayor. A synopsis in French was handed out to them. Before the performance, the mayor made a few remarks in French.

Later, Lea-Nour opened with *"Azafady tompoko!"*

These words were the formulaic way of politely getting listeners' attention and marked the beginning of a debate. Everyone got quiet, but there was stunned anticipation in the silence. Would they be speaking Malagasy before the foreign dignitaries? What was this young woman trying to provoke in breaking with decorum and disregarding gratitude, to boot?

The cultured Malagasy elite had readily given up their mother tongue. It was only natural in the presence of non-Malagasies, when following the code of cohabitation, which advised not to offend anyone, especially not a foreigner. But neither was it a rare occurrence for them to strive to maintain their French in private conversations. Perhaps this language allowed a wider freedom of tone; Malagasy seemed to oddly prevent any direct expression of disagreement. Thus, debates were usually livelier at the French Cultural Center than anywhere else. Even if, at the end of the day, the participants were still expressing, in French, their animosity toward the outside world beneath the arches on the Avenue de l'Indépendance, not exactly wanting to show internal conflict—a source of shame—in front of vazahas.

The young woman, however, with her honorable family name known by everyone, continued in Malagasy. She directly attacked the hypocritical society that was burying itself under a mountain of rules with the sole aim of perpetuating existing structures. Traditionalists and xenophobes were joining forces, she accused, and it happened more often than people wanted to believe, in their disregard for modern vitality, because both sides only ever praised copies and reproductions.

Lea-Nour harshly criticized the paradox of an insular culture that, either believing that it was open to the universal by venerating the dominant model in folklore and rejecting all uniqueness, or refusing all external aid and retreating into a nationalistic identity, would lead to only minor cultural disturbances, always intermittent and with no future to speak of. She wanted to encourage individuation that acknowledged their roots, encourage creation that could only be rooted, she clarified, in their most intimate selves.

"But we'll just be talking about ourselves!" someone objected.

"We can talk about everything," she countered, "because we've never said anything."

The confrontation was recorded and shown on TV. Lea-Nour's youthful energy and enthusiasm literally burst through the screen, and she soon became a muse for an informal movement of artists. Ietsy, idle and aimless, fell for this girl whom everyone else was idolizing. So, on a tip from Arthur, he went to a premiere that he knew she'd be attending, to bid his childhood friend a polite hello.

Other than each and every house, cardboard-city shacks, sheet metal slums, low-income hodgepodge housing, government apartments, traditional houses on the hills, grand villas in residential suburbs, schools, churches, tombs, and other places the spirit dwells, there weren't really any truly cultural spaces in the City of a Thousand Rites. Establishing a major cultural center, a project driven by a thousand organizations, was held in the highest regard by successive government administrations without ever receiving any financial follow-through. Politicians have always had a poor understanding of why culture matters, and it only ever holds an ancillary place in their long-term plans. Thus, when culture leaves the home, it occupies the streets and places financed by foreign delegations.

This event took place in the enormous parlor of an expat who had just returned to the country. It was an operetta of the legend of Ranour. The form called to mind the Ancients' dances under the full moon, where actors and musicians mixed into the audience, lambasted them, and they had to respond with fairly simple refrains, predictable exclamations, or pass summary judgments. The public played a full role that they learned as they went along. This went a long way in facilitating communication in other areas.

Lea-Nour had never expected to see Ietsy at such an event that, while it didn't fall entirely under the category of populist art, was intended to champion it. Ietsy unassumingly pretended to be interested in all rewritings of oral traditions, the legacy of the ears, as they said. She didn't know Ietsy had such interests, and the art lover laying himself bare before her was different from both the boy of her memories and the *No Fear, No Die* rumors that had spread through the City of a Thousand

121

Whispers. She discovered a multiplicitous being, like an onion, covered with ever more layers of itself.

Literature also brought them closer together. Ietsy used it as a safe passage to infiltrate discussions Lea-Nour went to, where artists and intellectuals usually re-created man and earth. "They're probably dreaming about a woman instead!" Ietsy whispered in Lea-Nour's ear. He took the opportunity to graze her proper bun with his temples and drink in her vazimba perfume. Ietsy's levity distracted her from the gravity of the ones reviving the Malagasy soul, which was still flying despite being completely weighed down by poverty and rancor. From one cultural hub to the next, he grew closer to his neglected playmate who'd become a very attractive young woman. He successfully got her to leave a session where all the wordmongers were religiously listening to themselves talk. Ever since, like rice and water, they could not be separated, in the city or the country. She trusted him, and he introduced her to exquisite pleasure.

"I looked at the blue sky and saw stars that no one else sees!"

"I stared at the earth, the pool of your eyes drew my gaze!"

They were good together. Two butterflies in a beam of light, different yet with equally dazzling wings, dancing together to a rhythm known only to them. The entire world conspired to get them together. But as much as love made Lea-Nour's eyes shine, it made Ietsy's heart stumble.

One day when they'd made love in the wild grasses of the Highlands and the sun went to hide jealously behind the clouds, she felt so alive with every part of her being that she told him so. Relaxed, satisfied, he laughed like a fool and kissed her plump lips, her defined cheekbones, her earlobes. She laughed too. Slowly, though, her words wormed their way into Ietsy and chilled him. They got up, walked around hand in hand. Both were distracted but for very different reasons. They got back to the motorcycle, and Ietsy hopped on. It was a motocross bike that he had to kick-start. Lea-Nour usually waited until the motor turned over to climb on. Ietsy started it but, lost in his thoughts, gave it gas and left without a backward glance. Incredulous, Lea-Nour couldn't say a word before he disappeared. There weren't cell phones there at the time, and they were in the middle of the countryside. Ietsy didn't come back until nightfall, after Mr. Razak, who'd come home relatively early, had brought him back to earth by asking after Lea-Nour. He got extremely worried and drove like mad. Fortunately, it hadn't rained that evening. When he saw her upset and mad, he didn't know what to say to earn her forgiveness except words that were strangely true and romantic. The magic moment they'd spent together that afternoon, he promised, had transported him into orbit, far from the earth. She believed him without showing it. He swore without lying at all. He got stuck trying to say more. To make her smile again, he told her with unexpected ardor that he wanted to tie the knot. A few weeks later, with his grandfather at the head of a procession of twenty family members and a professional orator, a renowned poet, he went to her parents' house to ask for her hand.

"The water's surface was smooth and blank, Mâ. The sky was reflected in it forever. There were no banks where any silver mountains or weeping willows were mirrored from. No papyrus or taro grew there. The sun blazed over the emptiness. Then it started stirring. As if a giant under the water was turning over in its sleep. Then I saw the enormous wooden birds floating on top. They must have broken their wings. Men stood there, women and children too. Not Ietsy's children, Mâ . . . They weren't carved from the same wood as us. One man was standing on the head of the largest bird. He was looking at me, Mâ! Then he turned to the people behind him, they looked lost on their wounded birds. They didn't move, their heads were bowed, dazed by the heat. None of them seemed to want to cool off in the water. As if they were afraid of the giant below . . . afraid that he'd wake, Mâ!"

The old Vazimba nodded her head slowly. While her young visitor, barely an adolescent, told her about her dream, she'd been carefully scrutinizing her face. She had no doubts of her sincerity. She'd watched her on the ravine path that led to her den. Despite her ordinary dress and sandals of vacoa stalks that seemed to carry her up the slope, the girl heralded nothing less in Mâ's eyes than something new coming.

"Where did you say your people were sculpted, my child?"

"The Sandy Glade, Mâ! My father has lived there forever. My mother, she's from Ambalavao. Her parents are silk weavers there. My father met her when he went to the market to trade his game. He brought her back to his forest straightaway. I was born there and haven't left, except to go to Ambalavao. This is the first time I've been so far away."

"Oh?"

"Yes, Mâ. Grandmother Ambalavao told me to come see you. I'm staying with her until the Festival of the First Fruits. I help her untangle the strings on her loom."

"Have you ever laid eyes on the sea, my child?"

"The sea? What's that?"

"It is the vast expanse of moving waters you dreamed about!"

"The sea?"

"Yes, the sea! Our earth sits in the middle of those swells—"

"The sea!"

"It's salt water—and have you had another dream since then?" The old Vazimba was getting carried away.

"Yes!" The visiting girl blushed. "I mean, I haven't dreamed of . . . Not like that . . . I saw the man again. The man who looked at me in the first dream. It was pouring down rain, and the man was looking up at the sky as it opened on his head. The more he got wet, the more he laughed. He made me laugh too."

"Hmm." The old woman nodded.

She was on her feet now, all excited, pacing around the girl, her thoughts aflutter. After circling around her twenty-seven times, she seemed to have put them in some order.

"Tell me your name again, sweet child!"

"Nour, Mâ."

"Nour, is what's happening to you unpleasant?"

"No, Mâ."

"You can go back home, Nour. I'll come to see you before the first fruits. But if you dream of the foreign people again, make sure you remember, when you see them all again, not just the man, do inform me."

Mâ watched as the young girl walked away from the threshold of her den, and when she saw her disappear around a bend in the path, she leapt into the air, danced around, and kissed the ground. Her joy was quiet. Since Ietsy, they had been making preparations for those who would answer the call. Mâ was one of the guardians of knowledge scattered throughout the island. It seemed likely that the event she'd been prepared for, she and her forebears for generations before her, would finally come to pass.

As Nour followed her shadow to return home, she hummed a tune she'd never heard before. Nothing surprised her anymore. Ever since the dream, the most unexpected things had been happening to her: the threads on the loom untangled themselves the moment she stretched out her hand toward them; the jug flew onto her head when she went to collect water from the spring, both on the way there and back; the local boys lowered their eyes when she worked chores with them; and at the market, men turned to look when she passed. She wasn't shedding her blood anymore at every moon. The fourth time, her grandmother had insisted she go see Mâ, the midwife. Nour actually found it rather nice. She knew she was changing, like a flower preparing to bloom. Her stomach was not rounding, but it didn't trouble her. After all, no matter what Grandmother had said, she'd only dreamed of the Stranger. The only slightly disorienting parts were the wet, engulfing emotions, new music, echoes of memory or tremors of a still-faint future. That didn't matter. Nour's strange sensations now had a name: the sea.

From the infamous afternoon in the countryside to the day of the wedding, Ietsy Razak was horrendously anxious. The people around him, including his fiancée, smiled about it, understanding it as the normal concerns of a man about to take an important step in his life. He knew exactly what it was he feared. He was on the brink of living again and didn't want to die. He only had to say yes. A matter of confidence. Of a virtuous cycle. He was scared of being scared, scared of betraying himself against his will. Of forgetting his future wife's name, an important meeting, the appointment with the tailor, or with the pastor to rehearse the ceremony, of failing in other ways like getting sick or losing the ring in one of his suit's several pockets. He tried to stay in the light. He did his best to make reminders for himself, he—who'd never used a calendar before—marked his to-dos on a big one beside his bed and crossed off the days. He tattooed Lea-Nour's name on his left arm. He even, for a time, gave up the freedom his bike afforded him, for fear of an accident. He watched what he said obsessively, what he ate and drank, even during his bachelor party. Néness was so disappointed that he made a speech about how they weren't burying the boy within him that night, but Ietsy himself. Ietsy didn't even argue with him. He was committed to keeping his word to Lea-Nour and trying to build a life with her.

The ceremony practically went off without a hitch. The only mishap had nothing to do with him, but the employees of faraway Orly Airport. Because of their strike, Boris couldn't arrive in time to be a witness. Arthur, never one to hold a grudge, stepped in. The delay, which Ietsy could have seen as a clear signal to stop the proceedings, only reassured him about his decision. Lea-Nour would prevent him from drifting over uncertain waters. Deep down he kept repeating, like a wise old man, that we don't get married because of love, but we love because of getting married.

During the *vodiondry*, the ritual offering of a sheep's hindquarters to Lea-Nour's parents, the question of their home was seen as a done deal on both sides. Anosisoa had long been lacking a woman's charm and children's shrieks. "Anosisoa will be revived," Mr. Razak said with pleasure. He asked only that the young couple agree to his presence in the main house for as long as it took him to set up quarters for himself above his offices. The families, delighted with the new ties to strengthen their old friendship, used the hurried arrangement to conceal Lea-Nour's growing stomach. The truth was that extramarital sex didn't offend as many people as it used to. Mr. Razak caused more astonishment when he draped the young couple in a lamba of wild silks.

"Everyone present here knows the tradition in Anosisoa," he said, getting straight to the point. "I myself did not break with it, but I have suffered enough from it to uphold it. I say now that, in this matter, if both parties are agreed, it will be the children who liberate their parents. In life, you will live in the same house; in death, you will remain in the same tomb."

Those in attendance, after a moment's hesitation, applauded the act. The in-laws had experienced Mr. Razak's grief and heartbreak at his wife's passing—at the time, the grandfather had insisted her body could not remain in Anosisoa, not only because of the ancestor's will, but also in order to give the young widower a chance to remarry. But he'd never taken that opportunity and instead, as he said, had suffered from the custom. This time, the grandfather said nothing.

Mr. Razak's unexpected words heralded a new beginning and proved to be the greatest blessing that Ietsy and Lea-Nour could have received. They would thus cross the bridge to Anosisoa together, united by a single lamba.

The strong, low heat removed all solidity from the ground. The air was heavy without suffocating. One hue flooded the universe. Sky and earth like the peel of an orange in the rays of the setting sun. Torpor melted over everything. Nothing moved. Even the speed of light slowed. Time had left, gone in search of another clime. It returned with a drunken sea, drunk on new land. Fresh land. Unsteadily, tenderly, the tide lapped at the passage to make it languid. Stubborn and unhearing, it went to leave the seed, the sacred offering, the bud that would sprout life. *Nour! Do you hear the rain outside?* The soaking, nurturing rain. The rain that brings laughter to the enlightened. That clear laughter, having burst from her dream several times already, made her heart thrill. Nour woke up gently, moving with a contented heaviness, her ears open to the song of raindrops on the roof. A humid, low heat bathed below her belly. It was as if the sea was lingering over her thighs, unwilling to ebb. Nour could hardly be surprised as she rose to find a gold-and-black seed on the shore of her bed. She held it between her fingers for a long time without being able to guess at the silent promise. Then, through the open doorway, a true daughter of the earth, she threw it into a puddle.

Lea-Nour's arrival in Anosisoa hardly caused any disturbance in the daily routine. The staff already knew her. She was used to having authority and, what was more, had the energy and education necessary to handle the responsibility of her people in return.

And besides, her work often took her outside. Ietsy supported her endeavors, went with her when she wanted him to, his flexible time and apathy adapting to her rather full life. She kept up her studies and dedicated her time to her passion for the arts.

"I feel at home here," Lea-Nour said.

"I love you," Ietsy said. "You are my life-giving water."

"I love you like the earth. In life, I am content to walk upon your back; in death, I will be delighted to rest within your breast."

Coming out of a socialist revolution, the country was giving a democratic revolution a go; soon those figureheads in power would understand they'd have to take part in a liberal revolution. The economy was collapsing under its debts, the culture under external donations. The forced march toward the empire of the market was crushing all unique qualities. Even the resistance itself was part of and getting diluted by that story of the world, which was steamrolling over everything else. Groups that called for a renaissance and worked toward cultural development by promoting the arts were sparking from small piles of kindling here and there. A little after the wedding, the one that had formed around Lea-Nour started to shrink around Anosisoa. Because of Anosisoa, of course.

In the last months of her pregnancy, Ietsy had wanted to ward off his wife's fatigue and, unable to move the university lectures, thought that at least the meetings that drew her away so often could be held in Anosisoa. The suggestion followed naturally from an idea that was already on the horizon, to push using national resources to support local culture; Anosisoa should have been an ideal place to bring the two together.

However, at the very first meeting, the splendor and ostentation made the other members of the group uncomfortable, even the artists and intellectuals from the upper crust. Just to get there, since most of them used buses and *bugsy*, the cooperative taxis teeming throughout Antananarivo, a car was waiting for them at the entrance to Anosisoa, which Lea-Nour sent at the last minute to take them over the two miles of private roads leading to the front door and transporting them into another world. The old housekeeper's formal welcome—despite her mistress's directive of simplicity, she could not or did not want to do anything less—the servants who couldn't be hidden, the furniture and place settings that couldn't be switched out for anything more modest, the high ceiling with sparkling chandeliers, they were struck by it all. They'd known the Razaks were rich, but they couldn't imagine all of this—they who lived in the crowded city in smaller houses, which the luckiest among them had inherited and partially rented out, but which were all in some state of disrepair that none of them had the means to restore, scrimping together even the smallest amount in savings to ensure their children's education, clothes, and yes, even their food (some of them would have loved to use just a few of the dishes served on the "no-frills" table in Anosisoa to spice up their family's white rice for the rest of the week), they experienced the country's debt in real life, working hard but bringing in barely enough to survive, they simply could not conceive of such magnificence. What they saw represented only a minuscule amount of the GDP that was being transferred abroad. But despite their clear-sightedness, even the most righteous among them could not help but associate Lea-Nour with how they were being exploited, and they lost confidence. As for the less right-thinking ones, they went to cherry-pick a few pieces of fruit before joining the others and, once their backs were turned, bad-mouthing the other freeloaders. As this sort of thing could not be discussed openly in the City of a Thousand Ambiguities, the participants slipped out one by one, offering fake excuses, and left Lea-Nour alone on her Enchanted Island with Ietsy.

"I'm sorry," Ietsy said.

"It was probably too soon!" Lea-Nour said with a smile, nestling up to him.

"I pushed your friends away."

"Oh, we were just unprepared."

Pregnancy concerns and her husband's increased attention distracted her from the defections. As she approached her due date, Ietsy started accompanying his wife to the university. Sometimes he went to the lecture halls with her, his dilettante mind appreciating the knowledge being doled out. Sometimes he waited for her outside, flying a kite—the Hill of the Mind, where the different colleges of Antananarivo were located, offered the perfect conditions for the toy he'd brought back with him from the park in Versailles.

That way, Lea-Nour could take a course on the literary contribution to Malagachization during the revolutionary period and smile when she spotted her husband's toy fluttering across the rectangle of sky left open for the students shut away inside. The professor's voice was like something out of a dream as he explained how a massive game was formed, centering around the writer E. D. Andriamalala, to bring new words into real life. They invented names for everything that the ancestors hadn't named or that had come later from the outside: from a taxi to mathematical terms, from the computer to parts of a truck.

The professor was analyzing the reception—or the lack thereof—of these neologisms on the street, people preferring to use foreign words to Malagasy ones, they took a "taksi" and used the verb "mi-invest," when Lea-Nour, standing instinctively and moving toward the exit, felt her water break right in the middle of the stairs. It spilled down the steps, splashing some students, spreading out in a pool below the flabbergasted professor's dais.

"She's going into labor," one of the female students announced.

"My husband is outside," Lea-Nour managed to say. "With a kite."

"I see a green kite," called another student, looking out the window.

"Is your husband's kite green?" the professor asked, trying to preserve a scientific attitude.

"Yes," Lea-Nour gasped.

Someone ran to get Ietsy. He left the kite with the campus street vendors' kids who'd been eying him enviously for a few days and raced toward the lecture hall. Lea-Nour was waiting outside the door. He got her into the car and sped away toward the Sisters' Clinic on the other side of the City of a Thousand Traffic Jams. She didn't give birth until late in the night. When they placed her mucousy daughter onto her chest, she radiated joy, still under the effects of the epidural, while an exhausted Ietsy collapsed at her side.

With the next two babies, he tried to get through it without excessive anxiety, accepted the help his mother-in-law offered, but each time it was as if he personally was fighting a battle to the death, as if the delivery table showed only superficial aspects of his silent internal struggle. And when Lea-Nour won, Ietsy was released. Don't they say that the breath of life takes root in love?

"I make my wife happy," he answered proudly when one of Lea-Nour's professors at a reception asked him what he did in life.

Mâ quickly dismissed the idea of sending a message to the Mother, mother to them all, daughter of Ietsy, Ratiakolalaina. Surely such momentous news warranted a council. And besides, no one knew anything about what would occur. Mâ watched the sun disappear behind the ridge above her. Sometimes, when the wind blew off the horizon like it did that evening, to die at the foot of her hill, the tops of the giant trees that stretched as far as the eye could see rippled, stirring like a green sea. The waves swept away the last clouds and brought the twilight with them. The darkness came from the earth and little by little took over the sky. The stars lit up like hopes for a new day. Just after, the moon rose. Mâ smiled at it.

After a simple dinner of grilled corn with honey, Mâ—flanked by her nighttime eyes, her old owl, Ghost-Sparrow, on her shoulder, and her obligatory fossa, a cross between a wildcat and a fennec—began the climb toward the Highlands. Her old bones couldn't tolerate long walks very well anymore. Her conversations with the Mother were draining from her memory like water in a whirlpool. She'd been delaying her pilgrimages to Tsievonana for years. That evening, it was as if the wings of youth had sprouted from her back. Following her hooting owl's instructions and accompanied by her fossa's cackling, Mâ worked her way up the path, steep and almost completely hidden under the ebullient vegetation, one step at a time. She was halfway up when the moon began its slow descent toward the west, hiding behind the other side of the ridge that remained for her to climb. Below her, the shadows slowly darkened the ground she had just covered. Her hill was only a small hump in the darkness. The wooded horizon still gleamed in the pale light of the sun she could no longer see, which seemed to withdraw in step with her climbing.

"Hoot, owl!" she cried. "Cackle, fossa! Show me the path to the Highland door!"

She continued her ascent, inexhaustible. She reached the highest point just in time to see the moon set, glowing red at the edge of the vast plateau. The mountain of silver glistened, still far away. She sat, looking at what she had just traveled, waiting for daybreak.

Behind the dark band of the forest, she could make out the sea, which would soon be set ablaze and deliver the sun. She took delight in imagining Ietsy alone at this window to the world, scanning the horizon, hoping for a few companions to arrive, and when that failed to occur, sculpting the ancestors of Mâ and all the Vazimbas still bereft of breath. So his messages had eventually fallen on interested ears. People were finally coming to visit them. Perhaps they would settle here! What an upheaval for the Vazimbas, new faces, exotic wood.

The first light of day burst from the horizon, starting as pearls of light crowning the peaks, then slipping down the verdant cascade to the treetops at the edge of the plains. The mist began to condensate and lift, shimmering, to brush the pale morning sky and withdraw to the horizon. Mâ stood and turned toward the mountain of silver that seemed to float in the middle of the land.

From time to time, Ietsy liked to do things "à la France": cooking for themselves, sitting down at the table without anyone to serve them, washing their own dishes. When that happened, they would gather in the serving pantry and eat a meal that Ietsy had prepared after being seized with the idea in midafternoon and giving everyone else the rest of the day off. That particular night, he prepared eggplant caviar from a Turkish recipe out of his encyclopedia of cooking, with lots of garlic, and an eel fresh from the rice fields.

"Why do you like France so much, Papa?"

"Because there aren't any little Vazimbas like you tugging on his ears or pulling his hair!" Lea-Nour teased as she tickled her younger daughter on the couch in the living room.

"Are we Vazimbas, Papa?" the youngest asked.

"At school, they told us they were savages who lived in caves and didn't know about iron or fire!"

"We're all a little vazimba!"

"Anosisoa is very vazimba!" Lea-Nour said.

"So wait, why isn't salt taboo for us?"

"Yeah, and Papa really likes garlic!"

"Me too. And I like Big Macs too!" the youngest said, remembering his vacation to the neighboring Réunion Island.

Everyone laughed. Without answering his children, Ietsy looked at his Ranour and thought that he was truly blessed by the Gods and Ancestors. He climbed onto the couch behind her. The children joined them and made a noisy, stationary parade. The youngest drove the family train.

"Didn't you like my eel?" Ietsy asked his youngest as he put him to bed.

"Of course I did, Papa. I love it when you cook."

Ietsy went back to his room, satisfied, and when Lea-Nour praised him too—"That eel was excellent!"—as she curled up to him (she was so good at fitting into his body, perfection as proof: she belonged in his arms), he basked in his happiness.

As his family had grown, he'd believed that he was securing his redemption. Especially once the boy was born, he watched him grow, seeing his own childhood again. One day, though, he also forgot his children.

For the Easter vacation, they'd rented a house with Lea-Nour's sister, her husband, and their only son in the spa town of Antsirabe. Near the end of the week, he took his three children and their cousin to a nearby lake. He was watching the children playing gleefully in the water when three tourists appeared.

They were riding unguided on horseback to Tritriva, the extinct volcano, about six miles from there. They asked him what route to take. Pleased to find someone who spoke their language, they got off their horses. They mentioned they'd seen a postcard of Lake Tritriva looking like an eye in the earth promising a rejuvenating bath. They'd heard it was very deep but that no one had really been able to measure it. To deter them from bathing in it, Ietsy told them the legend of the freezing green lake that now filled the volcanic crater. Two lovers were said to have flung themselves into it to live their love freely in the beyond, a love that their parents had forbidden on earth.

"The legend has foreign origins," he clarified. "When Vazimbas were the only ones populating this land, love was simple, lovesickness didn't exist."

Still, Ietsy told them about the tree whose branches were twisted in sorrow, which had grown at the very place where the entwined lovers were said to have jumped. If the branches were nicked, they ran with sap as red as blood.

While Ietsy was talking, one of the tourists, a woman, looked at him intensely. When their eyes met, Ietsy felt an odd prickling sensation on his neck. The others, who hadn't noticed a thing, were itching to go see the natural wonder. They invited him to come along. As if in a dream, he climbed onto one of the spare horses the tourists had been advised to bring, and he trotted easily next to the young woman in front. Their mounts' hooves raised clouds of red, at times almost pink dust. They had a lively conversation with lots of laughter. It was as if they'd known each other forever. Their companions whispered behind their backs and exchanged knowing smiles. The trip was long but not too difficult. The beautiful place repaid the travelers' efforts handsomely. On the way back, the other two complained of their aching seats. Ietsy and the woman, who seemed to be gliding instead of riding, also obligingly got off their mounts to stretch their legs. Both of their hands strayed from the reins to hold the other's, and their forgotten horses took full advantage of that to graze freely. "Aren't you forgetting something?" came the teasing voice of one of their companions. They turned to see their animals far behind them. They went side by side to collect them, sharing an undimmable smile. It was sundown by the time they got back to the edge of the lake where they'd met that morning. The children were waiting by the car, oddly well behaved. Crashing back down to earth, Ietsy said, "My children!" Then he and the woman parted from each other, after having joined hands for the last time. In the car, the children, the oldest of whom was barely eleven, stayed quiet. Perhaps they were upset with him, or just awestruck by their father's vacant look. They didn't talk about it at the house, either. Ietsy, the next day, was sore everywhere and nowhere all at once.

That's not to say it was the first time that Ietsy had felt temptation. He certainly wasn't lacking in opportunities. The girls of his youth didn't stop spinning in his circles the day he said yes to Lea-Nour. Other women presented themselves too. He just didn't want to see them. He was too preoccupied with the life he was building. He needed a solid foundation so as not to be engulfed within the shadows. No matter the cost, he tried to continue down the path he'd mapped out for himself when he'd made his commitment to Lea-Nour. Even if other images sometimes lived inside his head.

He'd seen Helen Jones on his only trip home from France during his studies. Néness had obviously told him that Arthur had gone to England, but he'd wanted to stop by to see his friend's mother, whom he'd sometimes thought of alone in his dorm room. He went to their house in the city, not far from Lake Anosy, and rang the bell. The housekeeper showed him to the sitting room while someone went to fetch Ms. Jones from her studio. She was hardly any different from his mental image. After they exchanged greetings, Ietsy admitted that he knew Arthur was out of the country. She seemed delighted and flattered by his visit.

"Sadly, I don't have much time to chat with you today," she said. "I'm getting ready for a show at the end of the week. Do you want to come to the opening?"

He gleefully accepted, but when the time they'd set to meet came, he was flying toward the summer skies of the Northern Hemisphere. Four years later, she was showing her latest works in the same gallery. Ietsy had seen the announcement in the paper while he was still on the plane with his father. He went straight there before even going to see his old friends.

As it happened, she was standing in the hall talking with another visitor. She was still just as beautiful. There were a few wrinkles around her eyes that softened the blazing fire of her gaze crowned by her red hair, which had given heat to the young man's teenage years. Ietsy, for his part, had bulked up, and he beamed with all the joy he'd staked on his return to the Land of the Ancestors.

"I'm a little late," he said, "but I finally made it!"

She looked at him blankly for a moment, then smiled.

"Hello, Ietsy! Arthur hadn't told me you were coming back."

"He doesn't know yet. I read in the paper that you were having a show, and I had to come right away."

"Are you that interested in my work?"

He said nothing and kept looking at her, his arms hanging slack. Clearly, he hadn't come for the paintings.

"I couldn't make it last time," he said again.

"You had to leave rather quickly, according to what I heard," she began.

Then, remembering what had been said at the time, and the words she herself had expressed, blindsided once again by this City of a Thousand Steps that she never stopped rediscovering, rejecting, and accepting, she couldn't stop herself from reprimanding him like a child.

"All the money your father gave the family couldn't bring that man back to life," she told him. "I hope it finally got your head on straight, at least."

Ietsy hung his head, feeling wretched. He was a head taller than her now, and he wanted to prove to her that he'd lived too.

"I came to see you right away," he ventured, "but I'm also planning to go see the family and apologize."

"Really?" she said, surprised. "I would very much like to be there for that."

"I'd love it if you'd agree to come with me," Ietsy said, startled not only by his boldness but also by his spontaneous idea.

They set the actual meeting for two days later. Mr. Razak, who'd believed the matter closed, didn't understand the purpose of the visit but, seeing his son's insistence, didn't stand in his way. After all, taking responsibility honored the young man.

"Bring Nestor with you," he advised, "no one knows you there!"

"All right," his son agreed, having avoided mentioning Ms. Jones's involvement.

He went to pick up Helen at her place in Anosy as they'd agreed. Uneasy with the task he'd given himself, even though his instinct told him he could earn the woman's respect through this act of contrition, Ietsy stood waiting for her in the sitting room, his mind blank. He didn't register her presence right away. Looking up at the back door, he saw her framed there, beautiful and radiant as ever, although soberly dressed. She smiled at him. It brought back Ietsy's smile and confidence instantly.

"I came on my bike," he said. "I brought a helmet for you, but if you'd rather not, we can take a taxi."

She was fine with riding on his bike. She put a jacket on, and her jeans hugged her slender waist. With the helmet, she could have passed for any one of Ietsy's girlfriends. The thought made him smile. But she didn't squeeze hold of him like they would have. The victim's family didn't live very far away. The motorcycle wove through the low streets in the Bikiraro floodplain.

When they stopped at the entrance to a narrow alley, Helen's white skin and red hair caused just as much commotion as Ietsy's wealthy demeanor, incongruous in that place. They roused more curiosity than aggression. Ietsy asked for directions. A boy in rags, like everyone else in the neighborhood, said he'd take them there while his playmate watched the bike.

"Keep a close eye on it," Helen told the young watchman in Malagasy, in front of the amused onlookers who'd started crowding around them.

She knew from experience that her knowledge of the language, along with the fact they were going to see someone who lived there, would ward off any possible ill intent. Ietsy was the least assured of the two. At that moment, he regretted that Thor wasn't there. As they made their way between

145

the slum walls of wooden planks and rusty sheet metal, single file, jumping over puddles of stagnant water, going around the piles of garbage, he didn't really know what he was doing there, or why. He turned around every so often to see how she was coming along. She smiled, which gave him back his smile. It became a routine. Neither one of them generally picked their way through these underneighborhoods. He offered her his hand at a particularly difficult spot. He didn't let it go until they made it.

He knocked on the wooden plank door with flaking paint. The middle-aged woman who opened it was concerned about what these important people wanted. She had a brightly colored scarf on her head and looked to be wearing several articles of clothing to conceal their tatters. Ietsy introduced himself as the one who had caused the accident. The woman was shocked; they could see in her eyes that she had been told it was someone else. However, since her late husband had never brought home as much money as he had in death, she said nothing and invited them in.

They walked into a tiny room. There was a lopsided table, two threadbare chairs, a crate with an old television set wrapped in cellophane on top, and another open crate with various tools inside. A staircase that was more like a ladder led upstairs. Made-in-China reproductions of landscape paintings hung on the walls, along with a photograph of John Paul II. The salvaged warehouse pallets that supported the whole structure poked through here and there. A door stood ajar, leading to a small yard where a charcoal stove was burning. She remained standing and offered them seats.

"I'm responsible for the accident," Ietsy said again to ease the woman's nerves. "I came here to ask for forgiveness."

The woman, made extremely uncomfortable by these distinguished guests who, what was more, were apologizing, muttered, paced around the room, and finally called to someone upstairs. A boy came down in shorts and a T-shirt that were so worn by repeated washings that their original colors were unrecognizable. After saying hello, he was sent out back, where he made himself busy.

"That's the little boy he left me with," lamented the woman.

"Doesn't he go to school?" Helen asked.

As always, the fact that she spoke the language eased the tension in the air. The woman complained about the academic fees, required supplies, and life in general for a widow like herself. She made beignets and sold them on the street. She'd been able to marginally expand her trade with other little things after she'd been awarded a sum from the accident, but since then she'd lost everything in the global recession. She'd even had to sell the new TV she'd bought at the time.

"But electricity hasn't made it to this neighborhood, anyway!" She sighed.

Then she went out back too. The two visitors sat stiff and straight in their chairs. Ietsy found the purpose of his trip again in Helen's smile. When the woman came back with her boy, carrying a steaming pot of tea and a plate of beignets, Ietsy, who'd actually come prepared, suggested a school in the next neighborhood, which his father subsidized.

"He won't have to pay for anything," he promised them. "He'll even receive a scholarship as long as he works hard."

"You hear what this man is saying?" the woman cried right in the boy's ear. "Tell the man thank you."

"Thank you, sir!" the boy said, bowing his head.

"I'm the one who must thank you for accepting my offer," Ietsy replied.

And again he asked them to forgive him. Although he'd come there because of Helen's beautiful eyes, he still secretly liked how the boy was glancing at him out of the corner of his eye, a mix of curious and grateful. He gave them more logistical details about the financial assistance, which the principal would disburse to them every month.

Helen was still smiling. They both thought the beignets were delicious. They finished their tea and bid them farewell. The woman thanked them again and called the ancestors' blessing down upon them. The boy walked them back to the motorcycle. Ietsy squeezed Helen's hand, which he'd taken again as soon as they went out the door. He'd thanked her as well. Helen had told him "well done" as a reward. On the bike, it felt to him like she was hugging him a little more closely. He followed a foul-smelling canal through the Palletville marshes. He was sad the ride was so short. In front of her house, she fixed her hair with one hand as the other gave him back his helmet. Ietsy plunged deep into her fiery eyes.

"I'm in love with you," he said.

Taken aback for only an instant, Helen laughed. It wasn't a teasing laugh. It was a surprised, alarmed, and delighted laugh all at once. It scared her for the very reason that it flattered her.

"Well, I love you too, of course," she replied, hesitating.

Then she quickly added, "You did a wonderful thing today! If my son did something like that, I'd be extremely proud." Seeing Ietsy's face darken, she brushed her fingers over his face, regarded his head, his shoulders, how he looked like a forlorn knight on his motorized horse, then opened her mouth as if about to apologize, but instead left without a word.

"Helen!" Ietsy yelled. It was the first time he'd called her by her name. She didn't turn around; she went through the gate to the back of the garden. Ietsy leaned his bike on its stand and chased her to her studio.

"I closed the door."

"I'm in love with you," he said again.

"How do you love me?"

The question stopped him in his tracks. He didn't remember the elders' answer for that silly game anymore. To sidestep the question, he repeated what he'd said, again and again, squeezing not Helen's hands but her arms in his arms, soon her lips with his lips. She twisted away and slapped him across the face.

149

"Do not force me!" she shouted. "Do you really think that's how a man behaves? You tear through someone's life and then come back four years later to beg forgiveness?"

And she turned on her heels and left, slamming the door behind her. He stayed in the studio, gobsmacked and his cheek burning. He tried to calm his breathing, surrounded by paint cans, brushes, pieces of canvas, parts of frames, and paintings. He savored his bitter failure with masochistic joy. As if his actions had been caused not by deep-seated feelings or desires but by an experience that, once accomplished, was almost a victory. As if he was still reascending his Andriba and reveling in every cannonball pounding through his illusions.

"I am a man, am I not? I am circumcised," he said to bolster himself as he turned the door handle. "There is no greater pain than that which I have already endured."

The late afternoon light that was streaming through the patio doors made him take another moment to breathe in the intimacy of the painter. Despite how cramped it was, this room, where he stood for the first time, seemed strangely empty to him. He felt an almost tangible absence. Then, remembering Helen's latest show of her works, he was amazed by the palpable wake they left in the studio.

Ietsy didn't see Helen again for the next three years, at least never in the same intimate setting as that day. Arthur had moved into his own apartment when he returned from England. Ietsy had tried very hard to reconnect with her, but she made sure she never spoke to him except when Arthur was present, at which point she treated him like a son. She would sometimes even reprimand him for the careless way he treated girls. His antics were no less lively as he worked his way through the Antananarivo bourgeoisie.

When she learned he was getting married, she called him up on the phone.

"I'd like to give you a painting," she said. "Come pick it out at the studio tomorrow afternoon."

"All right," Ietsy said, very surprised by the call.

He started picturing himself going to her house in Anosy again. He'd ring the doorbell, and Helen herself would come to the door. She'd lead him down the path to the back of the garden. It was the stormy season. It wouldn't have rained yet, but the clouds would have been gathering above the city all day, wrapping it in a warm, humid cocoon. Helen would be wearing a long, flared tunic dress, sleeveless and collarless, with green swaths over red and gray. Her bouncing steps over the stone pavers set into the lawn would reveal her ankles above her flat sandals. Once in the studio, she'd gesture toward a stool for Ietsy.

"I want to congratulate you," she'd begin. "Marriage is a commitment that honors the man and woman—"

"But you aren't married to your partner!" Ietsy would cut her off, not wanting to find out what point she was trying to make.

"True! We felt that our commitment was just between us, but it's the same thing. We've devoted ourselves to each other in the same way, for life, promise to become!"

"Promise to become!"

"Yes. Marriage is not just a commitment, it's also something that you build every day—"

"I know," Ietsy would interrupt her again. "I just think that's a nice turn of phrase."

Ietsy had made the decision to get married by himself. He didn't think Helen had anything to do with it. He didn't want her to lecture him about morals again. She would keep going anyway.

"Ietsy, every time I see you, you're with a different girl. I have to wonder if you understand that committing yourself to one specific girl means the end of all that."

"I know," Ietsy would repeat, standing up.

"Arthur told me that the day before you made this decision you still saw this as some trifling affair like all the others, and that now you don't even want to talk about it."

Ietsy would have started walking toward the door and would see the first raindrops crash against the windowpanes.

He'd want to fight back against what he saw as a personal affront, but this woman would have too imposing of a presence. He'd clam up like an oyster in its shell.

"Is it true?" she'd press.

He wouldn't know what the question was referring to anymore. Lightning would split the sky, and rain would pour down. It would be as if a dam had been breached somewhere in the sky. Soon, they wouldn't be able to see the nearby house. Ietsy would press his forehead on the other side of the drenched glass. It would cool him down without ridding him of his discomfort. She'd ask him why he was getting married, but he wouldn't hear a thing. The mask he'd crafted for himself would start to unravel, unable to hide any more misery. She'd take him by the shoulder. He'd turn and hide his face by squeezing her tightly. Overwhelmed by Ietsy's choked emotions, Helen wouldn't know what to say. She'd stroke his hair like a child. Then everything would shift. The touch of her bare arm, maybe, her warm body beneath the thin fabric of her dress, her perfume, would abruptly awaken old desires within Ietsy. He'd kiss her neck passionately, so close, holding her firmly in his arms. Her musky scent would fill his nostrils. She'd struggle against him half-heartedly. He'd seek out her lips as one of his hands gripped the bottom of her dress and the other kneaded her skin. He'd feel her resisting less, pressing herself to him, leaning her head back, more to bare her neck to him than to deny him her mouth. He'd caress her bare thighs as she returned his kiss. They'd make disheveled love, half-undressed, sweeping away tables and palettes, falling to the floor, crushing a roll of canvas. Then they'd undress each other all the way, each one breathing heavily, kissing all the while, Helen pulling her young lover to a couch in the back of the room, where they'd do it all again just as fervidly.

"Why do you want to get married?" she'd ask later, recovering.

"It doesn't have anything to do with you," he'd whisper, his lips relishing every pore of Helen's milky, freckled skin as if his life depended on it.

"Then take me again," she'd say.

A curtain of rain would cut off the studio from the rest of the world. She was approaching fifty then, twice his age. Their affair would last, even when their physical passion was assuaged, and give way to tender affection, just as secret. Helen's partner, the theater man, would notice, perhaps, but their open arrangement would prevent him from displaying any sort of resentment.

Ietsy was imagining his life moving forward with two women when Helen called him back.

"Come with Lea-Nour, of course," she said. "She has to like the painting too."

"Of course!" he said.

When Mâ reached the door to Tsievonana, the sun was only shining on the very peak of the mountain of offerings. She left her two companions at the edge of the woods encircling the center of the Vazimbas' world. The mountain of silver was reflected in the pool of tears from Ietsy's beloved, as always. Everything was bathed in bright blue. Visitors, enthralled, would instinctively start paddling in the air, as if they were already in the water. Even those who were accustomed to it would lose their footing a little before lowering their eyes so as not to disrupt their equilibrium, overly susceptible to the beauty of the eye in the earth. Mâ took a moment on the embankment to gather her thoughts. Then she placed her feet resolutely on the nearest lily pad, one after the other, and squatted down. The lily pad sank, and the eye in the earth engulfed Mâ.

There was, as they say, a flurry of activity. The undines, whom Mâ normally saw drifting slowly, were darting about, sparking and fizzing. Their eyes swept the depths of the lake like beams of light. Their flower-crowned heads perfumed the surface, the dreams of the children of Ietsy outside. "So, you do know!" Mâ said, once she was brought to Ratiakolalaina. And Ratiakolalaina smiled, taking her hand to lead her to a divan of lotuses.

"Your feet are aching, Mâ! I will massage them. Have you walked all day?"

"All day and all last night," Mâ said. "Joy gave me wings, and my fatigue vanished the moment your sacred water dampened me . . . Two days ago, a girl from Ambalavao came to see me."

"Yes," Ratiakolalaina urged.

Her ageless face lit up in a sweet smile. She lowered her head over Mâ and wrapped her feet in her long hair. With light pressure from her hands, she eased the guardian's feet.

"So, they are coming?" Mâ continued.

"Yes," Ratiakolalaina confirmed. "The first ones, and they seem to be having trouble." She continued her massage and inquired, "What is the girl's name?"

"Nour, Mother! She is as pretty as a tender banana leaf."

"Nour . . . Ietsy's joy!" pensive Ratiakolalaina translated. "We must make sure that this tender leaf does not fray. She is the only one who can bring them here safe and sound, thus fulfilling Ietsy's wishes."

"Very good, Mother. But you say these are the first ones?"

"They will come with the rising day. Others will come later, and some of Ietsy's children will depart."

Those were Ratiakolalaina's final words. The one whom Ietsy wanted to love in his final days on this earth went to join him. They still look down on us. The first ones came from the northeast. We hold that corner of our houses sacred in their honor: the first crop of our rice fields, the first drops of blood from our livestock, the first splashes from an opened bottle, we offer these things to the first ones in the northeast corner.

That was the direction Mâ took when she emerged from Ratiakolalaina's lake, her body unburdened of all fatigue, her feet stronger than ever, but her back stooped. The weight of all those years of solitude inherited from Ietsy seemed to have settled on her back, on the brink of the first meeting. Yet she did not worry, confident that tears of love would attract only lovers.

Upon reaching Ambalavao, she picked out the thatched hut where Nour lived from the fifty-two in the village because of the lotuses growing dreamlike on the doorstep. Magnificent flowers had burst open unabashed among the large leaves, as if bathed in the sweetest of waters. These lotuses were gold with spots of black, however, in contrast to the ones at the pool of love. Their beauty made the guardian stand straighter. After all, she had not come bearing bad news.

"Nour!" she called.

The very next day, after gathering all the lotus seeds, the two women left the village, escorted by a delegation of Vazimbas. Other children of Ietsy, more and more, came to join them, called in dreams by Ratiakolalaina's nymphs. Nour, with her old shoes and her sack filled with black-and-gold seeds, seemed to glide over the path to the sea.

With her children sitting around her, Lea-Nour told the story once again, of how the first ones to answer Ietsy's call reached the Great Island after traveling thousands of miles in their huge outriggers and finished the crossing by walking on giant lily pads that Nour, the young Vazimba, made to grow as she went out over the water to meet Gola's fleet. Ietsy Razak also listened, as enchanted as his children, to the story he knew by heart, his head buried in Lea-Nour's hair, inhaling her scent of perfumed earth. He felt like he was once more opening a new drawer in the huge chest of mythology.

With his wife, he put his children to bed, their eyes closing under their kisses, already misty with dreams. Then he watched Lea-Nour getting ready for bed, thinking of how he would not be sleeping that night.

"Are you going to come to my first class tomorrow?"

She had just gotten a position as an associate professor in the literature department at the University of Antananarivo. At thirty-five, she'd managed to complete her coursework and dissertation in record time, if everything were taken into account: the frequent strikes by teachers, administrators, students, or more often the whole university, plus her private life, her marriage and children, whom she dedicated lots of time to.

"What are you lecturing on?"

It was the month of October, the end of the southern winter, jacarandas blooming. The early risers, or anyone like Ietsy who didn't sleep, could look out on the mist under the paling sky as it lifted from the rice fields and, when it reached the hilltops on the eastern edge of the Antananarivo basin, met the first light of the day. The City of a Thousand Pink Brick Walls stirred with various greetings, the rare crows of roosters who slept in late more often than not, the gentle swishes of washing, and the diffuse smoke from the first meals, before the motors started to roar, taxis, bugsy, the urban buses and regional taxi-Bs, and before the crowds started to pour into the main thoroughfares downtown and in the ministry districts, into the narrow streets twisting through the underneighborhoods and the paved lanes up in the hills. The springtime sun washed over the City of a Thousand Hives as they deployed over a thousand open-air markets, the produce merchants setting out their fruits and vegetables in their stalls, the butchers their meat, the flower sellers their flowers, the traders their various wares, the secondhand booksellers their secondhand books, the fabric sellers their fabrics, the druggists their drugs, the catchall men everything they'd caught plus their portable phone in their car parked in a spot on the Avenue de l'Indépendance. Here, you can find anything at any price until the daytime star begins its slow descent. Then all at once it rushes back, retreating to the bowels of the earth where it sucks away all the pollution, sponges out harsh colors in cunning shadows. Then the sky once again pulls on its dress of black velvet scattered with stars, a zebu's stretched skin, the poet says, while on earth, the plants exhale their perfume, freed by the gentle night.

"Love in contemporary literature," Lea-Nour answered, snuggling farther under the quilt. "Leave the window open so we can hear the crickets a little."

"Are you going to talk about *The Hamlet of Dreams*?" Ietsy asked, sitting at her feet.

She nodded, smiling. She'd done her thesis on E. D. Andriamalala, a romantic idealist who built and rebuilt a home for Malagasy literature, endlessly dismantled and burned to the ground. He was obsessed with one woman, pursuing her through each of his works until his masterpiece, where he made her an extraterrestrial who appeared to him with different faces. His love in *The Hamlet of Dreams* would come from the heavens, safe from earthly depravities, selfishness, and death.

"I'll be there." Ietsy guffawed as a crescent moon rose over Anosisoa. "That Andriamalala stuff might even be able to make me fall asleep!"

"Don't make fun," she said, still with a smile. "No one paints the infinite nature of love better than him."

"That doesn't exist," Ietsy blurted out, the words popping out of his mouth of their own accord. "Love, more often than anything else, ends. The thing that makes it seem to us to transcend all else is that when it dies, those who had it in their lives become like dead men. It's like life itself is leaving us, you can want to die for real."

As he said all that, face haggard, eyes red from all those hours without sleep, Lea-Nour watched him and listened to him, mouth agape, assailed by conflicting emotions. It was as if she was faced with not her husband but some stranger. He was being mean, almost sadistic. Then, behind the pallid, cynical mask, she glimpsed a more tormented Ietsy. Her sustained smile was fighting a courageous battle against the mounting sadness within.

"No one talks about these things." Ietsy was raising his voice. "But everybody knows it. We'd rather—"

"Ietsy!" Lea-Nour murmured softly, placing her finger on his lips.

She'd sat up and drawn near to him, stroking his face and hair, holding him close. Her hands and lips took turns to keep Ietsy's mouth closed. Yet old sighs still escaped from his lips, as if answering the house's creaking wood, seemingly roused by the mild temperatures.

The fragrance of evening jasmine filled the room in large puffs. Lea-Nour knelt on the bed holding Ietsy in her arms, her long, silky hair covering his face, buffeting the tears that were being wrenched from the very depths of the man's heart in mute, endless sobs. The clock above the stairs finished chiming ten o'clock and continued to measure each second. Crickets chirped above the night's whispers. An owl hooted somewhere. Pipistrelles darted across the light that fell outside from the bedroom's open shutters. Trucks, probably returning from trash collection in regions far and wide, rattled the Anosisoa bridge, adopting its creaks and groans. Once in a while, dogs barked far away.

"Shh," she breathed in his ear.

Ietsy woke up. The first thought that came to his mind was that he'd finally slept; then, that it was warm. He heard the children playing in the attic. So, he thought in confusion, they were already home from school. Pushing himself up to sit, he glanced at his wife's alarm clock in a panic: sixteen hours had gone by! He'd slept. A whole night, and the next day too. He'd missed Lea-Nour's class.

He rushed to the shutters and cautiously cracked them open. A ray of light dove into the dim room and cut it like a blade into two dark sections. People he couldn't see were talking outside: his in-laws' voices, they were on their way out. The children were being called. As he listened to them racing down the staircase, his eyes caught sight of the lily pads skimming the tiles of the swimming pool, the pink and white lotus flowers unabashedly opening their petals in the unnaturally blue water. Ietsy stared motionless at the outlandish tableau. He refused to make even the slightest movement, for fear of activating his neurons. He heard a car drive away from the front steps, then nothing. Without taking his eyes off what was certainly some sort of miracle, he heard terror settle over his heart like the silence in the house.

After a long time he managed to turn away. He opened the bedroom door. Everyone seemed to have deserted the house. He walked downstairs slowly, then faster and faster. He went through the living room, popped his head into the library, didn't see anyone. He hurried toward the serving pantry, not a single living soul, reached the kitchen and swung open the door to the outside. He got carried away by his momentum and almost fell flat on his face in the vegetable garden. The servants, who at that hour were usually taking their break in a schedule determined from the dawn of time, were not chatting there on the bench along the wall outside, awaiting their masters' impromptu desires. He ran past the empty veranda, passed the glass doors of the playroom, also empty, and turned the north corner of the house, his heart pounding like a dream.

The pool still had the surrealist water plants he'd seen from the bedroom window. Lea-Nour was gazing at him. She was waiting for him, seated on the steps, up to her chest in water.

"Lea-Nour!" he cried.

"Yes?"

"I slept," he said.

"Now you're awake," she said, standing.

She was wearing a dress with bright green, almost yellow ruffles. She walked into the pool, and a corolla of sun formed around her. Ietsy screamed, "No!" but he didn't even hear himself. Lea-Nour continued into the water. When there was only her head above the water, she stared at him with her black eyes and bid him farewell. "You're awake, but it's too late!" she mourned. And she plunged in. Ietsy couldn't feel his legs anymore; he collapsed onto the ground and crawled to the edge of the pool. The dress was floating in the middle of the water lilies. The colors, all wrong, seemed to be mocking him, every fragment of light tearing his heart to shreds. He closed his eyes in despair.

After an eternity of falling endlessly into darkness, someone shook him.

"Ietsy! Ietsy!" they called. "It's getting late."

Ietsy opened his eyes to see his housekeeper opening the windows of his bedroom.

"Madame's class begins in an hour!" the old woman said.

When those words reached his brain, when he understood, he looked gratefully at her and leapt out of bed. "Thank you, Marie!" he said, surprising himself by calling her by her name. A few minutes later, the blessed one crossed the rickety bridge from Anosisoa and hurried to the university.

EPILOGUE

So, might I be allowed to hope that people would retain my two inventions?

In short, it is still nonsense. To think that the meeting would come about just from tugging on a thread that asks only to be unrolled from nothing, and which would, once so delivered, be absolute proof.

The other evening, we were at a club to celebrate the birthday of one particular dear friend of mine, Ietsy's sister-in-law. Ietsy was there, seated, head cocked, resplendent, like one of his forebears whose engraving graces a page in our schoolbooks, all in white, his straight hair cut mid-length to round his already pleasant face: a thread ball unrolling to golf shoes on the nightclub's armchairs.

What were they again?

> —*Men do not cry; they are contemplating Ietsy's pool.*
> —*Enchanted as Ietsy was, buried in the land of his children.*

ABOUT THE AUTHOR

Photo © 2019 Sophie Bazin

Born in Antananarivo, Madagascar, Johary Ravaloson is an author and publisher living in Normandy. *Return to the Enchanted Island*, his first novel to be translated into English, won the Prix du roman de l'Océan Indien. In 2006 he founded Dodo Vole Publishing with his wife, contemporary artist Sophie Bazin, starting a new trend of in-country publishing in Madagascar and Réunion. Ravaloson is also the recipient of the 2016 Prix du livre insulaire and the 2017 Prix Ivoire for Francophone African Literature for his novel *Vol à vif*. His latest book released in French is *Amour, patrie et soupe de crabes*.

About the Translator

Photo © 2015 Devon Rowland

Allison M. Charette translates literature from French into English. She has received an NEA Fellowship in literary translation and a PEN/Heim Translation Fund Grant, been selected for the Translation Lab residency at Art OMI, and been nominated for the Best of the Net. Her translation of *Beyond the Rice Fields* by Naivo, the first novel to be translated from Madagascar, was published by Restless Books in 2017. She founded the Emerging Literary Translators' Network in America (ELTNA.org), a networking and support group for early-career translators. Visit www.charettetranslations.com.